P9-DXE-627

FICTION

ATLANTIC
MONTHLY
PRESS

SAD

MOVIES

SAD

MOVIES

a novel by
Mark Lindquist

THE ATLANTIC MONTHLY PRESS
NEW YORK

Copyright © 1987 by Mark Lindquist

All rights reserved. No part of this book may be
reproduced in any form or by any electronic or
mechanical means including information storage and
retrieval systems without permission in writing from
the publisher, except by a reviewer who may quote
brief passages in a review.

FIRST EDITION

Library of Congress Cataloging-in-Publication Data

Lindquist, Mark, 1959–
Sad movies.

I.–Title.
PS3562.I51165S2   1987   813'.54   87-15286
ISBN 0-87113-173-0

Published simultaneously in Canada
Printed in the United States of America

First printing

Design by Laura Hough

ACT

I

I wonder why I don't kill myself?

I wonder why I'm wondering, then tell myself not to think like this and light a cigarette instead.

It's about three A.M.

I stand here in the bedroom of my apartment trying to make the things go away by looking out the window at the ocean and the almost full moon and listening to the rhythm of the waves.

"I thought you wanted to go to bed?" Becky says from the bed in a very sweet sexy way.

I don't turn to face her.

"Well?" she says.

"No."

She sort of laughs. "No, you're not well? Or, no, you're not coming to bed?"

"Both."

"I thought you wanted to get some sleep."

"I do."

"Standing up?"

Pause.

"Horses do it this way," I say.

"Horses also have sex that way."

I know she's smiling.

The problem, *one* of the problems, is that I *do* want to sleep. And this worries me.

There's a party in the other room of my apartment and there's Becky in this room and all I really want to do is lie down alone and sleep for an eon. And with a history of lunacy in the family I'm afraid this makes me closer to my roots than I'd prefer.

"I am the way, the truth, and the life, no man's soul cometh unto the Father, but by me!"

On the boardwalk below my window one of the neighborhood characters walks along screaming this very thing. He's wearing a diaper and carrying around a ten-foot wooden cross.

"I am the way, the truth, and—"

"You're insane!" I yell out at him.

"Who are you yelling at," Becky asks.

"The drunk with the cross."

"Oh," Becky says, "him."

"I am the way, the—"

"Prove it!" I yell.

He doesn't look up at me. Maybe he thinks my soul is beyond hope. I don't blame him.

I try to focus on the ocean. The biggest body of water in the world. Suddenly I decide I don't believe in evolution. Can't decide what to order at the sushi bar, but I'm quick with the Big Questions.

I wonder what I do believe in.

"What are you thinking?" Becky asks.

"What?"

"What are you thinking about?"

I shrug and toss my cigarette out the window and

watch it twirl through the dark. Before it lands I light another.

I don't know what I believe in.

But I know it's out there. The Plague. And I know I'm not the only one who sees it. I know the people partying in the other room are either talking about it or around it.

I can hear them, the ones who feel it's sacrilegious to leave a party before it's light outside, and though because of the volume of Siouxsie And The Banshees I can't make out exactly what's being said, I can still hear the usual: movies and money and commercials and TV and herpes and AIDS and terrorists and nuclear holocaust and laughter.

I go to the portable tape player and turn on whatever's already loaded. "*. . . I find it kind of funny, I find it kind of sad, the dreams in which I'm dying are the best I've ever had . . .*" Tears For Fears, naturally. This drowns out the sounds from the other room.

"Come to bed," Becky says.

I turn to face her. She's sort of smiling and her body is barely tan and her small breasts are white. I'm a beaten man. I retreat under the sheets but Becky pulls down the sheets, and my boxers.

Two nudes mounting in the moonlight.

△

It isn't working.

We keep trying.

Desperate kissy, kissy, touchy, touchy, pant, pant, pant, sigh, and the cassette plays out and the pleasure turns sour and we both accept the fact that Zeke Junior isn't coming up to play tonight.

5

I light a cigarette and stare at the ceiling while we listen to the feedback of The Jesus and Mary Chain's *Psychocandy* playing in the other room.

"You're pretty drunk," Becky says nicely.

"Not *that* drunk."

"No?"

"No."

"Well . . ."

"And I was dead sober last night."

"Last night I thought sobriety was the problem." She smiles in the dark.

Thank God for her smile. Becky smiles and suddenly all the ugly aggravations seem as stupid and absurd as a rock video.

I remember her once saying when you're in love nothing else matters. I asked if this was courtesy of the new Sting album or a poster of dandelions. Still, I had to admit it was a nice idea. Just not out loud.

"Zeke, do you want to talk?"

"About what."

"Whatever's bothering you."

"What's bothering me?"

"I don't know."

"Neither do I."

I want to talk. I just don't know what to say.

"Maybe you should have another drink," Becky suggests.

Though she's only joking, I get up and walk naked into the kitchen and help myself to a J&B on the rocks while the few remaining partyers pretend not to notice my nakedness and babble on about whether herpes and AIDS are signs from God or just rotten luck.

I think about telling them to leave, but then

6

decide I don't want to break up whatever's keeping them together, so I don't.

I come back with the drink and sit down next to Becky on the bed. We share it as we both smoke. Me, nonfiltered Camels. She, Camel Lights. I think we probably look like a cigarette commercial. It's sick.

The bond—the connection, the vague whatever that keeps her from leaving or bludgeoning me to death—seems to build back up in our silence.

Someone in the other room takes off The Jesus and Mary Chain and puts on the Smiths and cranks the volume.

". . . *I am human and I need to be loved, just like everybody else does. . . .*"

I listen for a while and think this sounds much better now than the first few times I heard it. I wonder what my neighbors think.

"I'd like to talk," Becky finally says.

"About what."

"Anything," she says. Becky can turn an innocent word into an emotional avalanche. This worries me. One of the problems of living with a twenty-two-year-old actress is the chronic fear she's acting.

"Okay," I say. "Let's talk."

Pause.

"Do you want to take a blanket to the roof?" she says.

I shake my head and think of all the dark nights we've lain under the stars and made up stories about the civilizations in far-away galaxies. Becky imagines Utopias. I imagine living hells.

"A midnight drive? By the airport?" she says.

I shake my head again and think of our nights in

7

Playa Del Rey in the parked convertible having good desperate sex under the planes coming in to land.

"Some porn on the VCR?"

I really shake my head and think why the fuck would she say that? I look at her and she's smiling.

"A joke," she says.

"Yes."

"Since you think porn movies are so funny."

"They *are* funny."

"I think they're good inspirational entertainment," she says. "Just like the Bible."

"You should quit watching TV evangelists."

"They're better than Wally George."

"*Anything's* better than Wally George."

" 'Star Search'?"

"Okay," I admit, "*that's* worse."

" 'Lifestyles of the Rich and Famous'?"

"Why are you torturing me?"

"Judith Krantz novels?"

"I've got to go to sleep," I say, putting out the cigarette.

"But we're talking," she says. "This is our first talk in a week."

"We're not talking, we're bantering."

"Bantering is conversational foreplay," she says. "I think you told me that once."

I deny ever saying any such thing and kiss her good night.

We lay silently for a while, music filtering in from the other room. *"You say it's going to happen now, but when exactly do you mean? See, I've already waited too long and all my hope is gone. . . ."*

I know there's no way in hell I'm going to fall asleep. Thoughts repressed by day revolt by night.

I go to the bathroom and get a couple Valiums from one of the several prescription bottles I took from Mother long ago. Back on the bed I wash the ten milligrams down with the Scotch.

I wait for the numbness to take hold.

"Do you want a back rub," Becky asks.

"You're a genius."

I lie down. Her hands start with the back of the head and neck, talented hands, working down to the small of the back where her touch lightens, and on all the way to the soles of the feet.

"Heaven . . . heaven . . . heaven," I mutter at random intervals.

"Sssh," she says. "Relax. Everything's going to be okay."

"Bullshit."

"Sssh," she repeats, laughing. "Go to sleep."

I finally feel myself falling asleep in the smog-blue light of the coming L.A. sunrise.

"Happy twenty-fifth," I think I hear her say.

△

Loud static, then—*"They're after you with their promises, promises of love . . ."*—the radio/alarm tuned to KROQ goes off.

I stumble blindly into the bathroom, pick up a tube of shampoo, and proceed into the shower where for expediency's sake I urinate.

I start rubbing the shampoo into my head, but when there's no lather I realize it's suntan lotion. Though I should laugh at this, it almost makes me snap. I sit down under the shower stream and let it rain on me until it starts to get cold.

As I dress I admire Becky. She's turned off the

radio/alarm and appears to be asleep. Skinny girl with full lips. I can't decide whether the dark red coloring of her sealed lips is natural or leftover lipstick. I feel like I should know.

"You're a goddamn gorgeous angel," I say.

Becky makes an animal noise and rolls over.

I put on the usual: un-ironed khakis, un-ironed white button-down, and L. L. Bean moccasins. I haven't the motivation to explore new sartorial territory. I don't tuck in my shirt because I'm tall and the shirt will untuck itself eventually and what the hell difference does it make?

In the kitchen I put water into Mr. Coffee and since I still feel like hell I add some Scotch as well. I spend about two minutes trying to chew a couple granola bars, then swig down a cup of Mr. Scotch Coffee with a handful of vitamins and I'm ready to go to the office.

But I can't find my Ray-Bans. The horror.

I search the usual obvious places including my coat pockets and still can't find 'em and I end up in the middle of the apartment frustrated and confused.

I decide if I can't find my sunglasses, the office will have to wait.

Then I decide to give up looking.

I feel better already. My body is begging for a good breakfast so I open the refrigerator to check supplies. There are my goddamn sunglasses right next to the tomato juice.

"Fuck."

Can't fight fate.

△

I get my morning workout by lowering the broken rag-top by hand. As is expected of a Late-Empire American convertible, it is slowly falling apart.

This morning, like so many mornings, some quasi-religious group has left a pamphlet on my car window that promises doom and offers hot hints on salvation. I save it in my glove compartment with all the others.

I join the flow onto the Santa Monica Freeway smoking and coughing and crawling with the crowd in smoggy morning traffic. On the radio there are too many commercials, and this incredibly un-hip deejay with an Australian accent is speaking as if we must be as stupid as he is since we're listening to him and so I put on a tape of a local band, X. *"I must not think bad thoughts, what is this world coming to. . . ."*

I can feel my muscles tense up.

My conscience is complaining about the work I'm going to do today. I tell my conscience to shut up and join the modern world.

I have a dream: to get through the goddamn day. Get through the goddamn day without becoming murderous or suicidal or worse.

Dreams are cheap in this town.

△

Big Gun Films' offices occupy the top six floors of a shabby building in a seedy section of Hollywood. Everything about Big Gun Films is shabby and seedy. The industry standard is mediocrity, but Big Gun Films try harder.

Two Arabs and a West L.A. Mercedes dealer bought this small company that specialized in low-budget youth flicks and did the impossible—*lowered* the quality of product. The drop in quality corresponded to a rise in profits, of course.

Big Gun then merged with a pharmaceuticals

outfit. But for corporate reasons I don't understand, or want to understand, the Arabs and the Mercedes dealer maintain a controlling interest in Big Gun Films. The only effect the merger has had is that all Big Gun movies plug the right brand of aspirin, deodorant, toilet paper, and so on.

There are a few directors with integrity who won't work this way. At Big Gun, however, this is not a problem—they hire only shameless hacks.

My job is to write bad copy for bad movies.

I have this job because after college graduation I spent almost a year getting drunk in Europe, and when I got back to L.A. I wasn't exactly overwhelmed with employment offers, and a guy I went to U.S.C. with said he could get me in the door at Big Gun. I thanked him. I was relatively innocent and didn't know better.

I get to the office today, my normal hour late, and Peg calls to tell me I have to rewrite my poster copy for *The T Team,* a movie about nine Las Vegas showgirls recruited as an antiterrorist rescue squad.

Peg, who rose to her position as Vice-President of Marketing and Advertising by virtue of an affair with the Mercedes dealer, tells me my initial effort wasn't up to my old standard.

The owners of Big Gun don't know much about making American movies, but they do know how to make money in America—by advertising, so they personally approve or disapprove all copy and design. Peg tells me my contributions haven't been going over well with the big boys lately. I feel like telling her my contributions have been going over their foreign heads, but I remember today's dream—*get through the goddamn day*—and I tell her she'll have some truly genius copy on her desk by the end of the day.

I shake my head and wonder why I'm using the word *genius* this way.

She asks how my other assignments have been coming, the usual lies about actors and directors that are sent out to the media so some lackey at some magazine or newspaper or TV station can pick up the P.R. and generate free publicity for the movie being pushed.

A Xerox of my best bio work is taped on my desk:

"He's young and he's a movie star and his life is unbelievably bitchen. You should want to be one, too. Being a movie star means never having to take a shit."

Nobody ever commented on this when the bio went out. Maybe they all thought it was true.

I tell Peg everything's fine, thank you.

She scolds me for recurrent tardiness and I warn her I'm in the wrong mood for the usual bullshit. My tone must be severe, because Peg, who's not exactly famous for respecting employee feelings, says, "It's okay, Zeke, it's okay," and then says she's looking forward to my new copy for *The T Team.* I hang up and laugh.

I stare at the blue Selectric. I type:

> *The T Team is Coming*
> *In A Multiple Caliber Climax*

I know it's bad, but wonder if it's bad enough. I try something shorter:

> *An Ecstatic Adventure*

Something longer:

> *They Come In the Country as Dancers*
> *They Come Out as Killers*

"Enough of this shit," I say.

13

I go to the coffee room and munch on cheap granola bars the company provides. I remember my first week of work I walked in here and one of the lights went out. That was six months ago, and it hasn't been replaced yet. I decide not to think about this.

I smoke a cigarette and watch the coffee maker drip while some secretaries come in to gossip about Madonna and Sean and the new sodomy laws. I have nothing to say on this subject. So I go to the men's room and sit in a stall and smoke more cigarettes while I read the graffiti and I find myself laughing at this one line scratched into the wall:

THEY'RE KILLING ME

Someone else has written below this in pencil:

WHO?

I decide to scratch in an answer:

YOU KNOW WHO—THEM!

Eventually I wander up to the art department to seek inspiration from the poster for *The T Team* and to see Wendy and Susie.

"Zeke!" Susie yells.

"Close the door," Wendy says.

I close the door and walk over, passing the cubicles of other artists who are either sketching or sleeping or, this early in the morning, sleeping somewhere else.

Wendy and Susie are sitting together in Susie's cubicle. Little Wendy is wearing nothing but black and she's smoking a cigarette and looking bored. Big Susie is wearing about twenty pounds of chains and icons and she's smoking a cigarette and appears to be working on a poem.

These two are part of the reason I can keep returning to this daily depraved aggravation. These two plus my heavy credit card debt.

Some of Susie's poetry from last month is still written on the wall above her drawing board with black El-Marko pen:

> *why have a boat*
> *when you don't have a dock*
> *why have a dick*
> *when you don't have my twat*

Below this in smaller letters is my response:

> *why holiday at niagara falls*
> *when you can stay home*
> *with my blue balls*

"Why hasn't anyone cleaned that up yet," I ask.

"It's poetry," Susie says.

"It's *embarrassing*," I say.

"I'm not embarrassed," Susie says.

"The world *needs* beautiful thoughts like that," Wendy adds.

"Yeah," Susie says.

I nod and light a cigarette.

"Have you had any new revelations you want to write down," Susie asks.

"No," I say. "I'm here on *The T Team* mission. Where's the poster?"

"You want to see it now?"

"Whenever."

"Let me finish this first," Susie says and taps out the rhythms of her poem and writes the word *penisbrains*.

"How was the party last night?" Wendy says.

15

I shrug.

"Sorry we couldn't make it."

"Was there an orgy?" Susie wants to know.

"Naturally," I say.

"*Really?*" Susie says.

"No," Wendy says.

"How do you know?" I say.

"I know," says Wendy.

"Why do I always believe you, Zeke," Susie asks.

"I don't know."

"Susie!" some guy yells, "could you toss me your T-square?"

Susie hurls her T-square at him and he ducks and it flies by and gashes a Brooke Shields publicity poster. This fazes no one.

"We *wanted* to come to your party," Susie says, turning back to me, "and we were on our way but we ran into these guys at the Kitty Box Room, and they had coke, and then, after—"

"—Oh, that's *right,*" Wendy cuts in. "We have a gift for you, Zeke. Come on."

Wendy grabs her purse and Susie wads up her poem and throws it in a wastebasket.

"I should see that poster," I remind them as we walk out.

"I did that one," Susie says. "It's way cool."

I follow them down the hall into the developing room. Wendy locks the door and turns on a red light and takes out a little mirror and starts cutting lines.

What's left of my senses is begging me not to do it.

"God," Wendy says, "I hate working here."

"There's so much negative energy here," Susie says, "I feel it's sucking on me like that creature in 'Star

Trek.' Have you seen that one? With the creature that disguises itself so you'll come close, then turns back into itself—this really ugly octopuslike thing that sucks everything out of you."

"Yes," I say, "I've seen it."

"That's what it feels like to me."

"I feel like I could get fired any second," Wendy adds.

"Me too," Susie says.

"I can't imagine why anyone would fire such diligent drones," I say.

They both nod as though I've made a good point.

Wendy hands me a straw.

My nose tissue whimpers.

"Happy birthday yesterday," she says.

For the ritual, not the high, I hoover up a line and hand the straw to Susie, who does the same and passes the straw to Wendy, who does the same and passes it back to me.

"I've got to come up with some killer copy for *The T Team,*" I say.

"How about 'Don't See This Fucking Stupid Exploitative Potentially Brain Damaging Movie,' " Wendy suggests.

"That's good," Susie agrees.

"Very good," I say, "but I have this horrible feeling my job is on the line. I don't know why, but the guillotine seems to be trembling in the air."

"Bullshit," Wendy says, "Peg loves you."

"Loves you." Susie nods.

"I can't imagine why," I say.

"She's a sucker for good-looking guys," Susie says.

"I'll remind her of that when she fires me," I say and have another line.

"If heads roll," Wendy says, "It will be ours."

"She won't fire you." Susie takes her line.

"You'd be lucky if she did," Wendy says, taking hers. "But she won't."

Wendy wipes her finger across the mirror and then pokes it in her mouth while Susie wipes her finger across the mirror and pokes it in *my* mouth.

We look at the empty mirror for a few moments.

"Didn't you want to see the poster for *The T Team*," Susie asks.

I nod.

As we walk down the hall, Susie tells Wendy and me about yesterday's episode of the "Brady Bunch." "Jan's getting pissed off about having such an overpopulated family, about sharing shit with *every*body, and she gets to be such a *pain* about it, saying she wishes she didn't have five billion brothers and sisters, that the other kids come up with this plan."

Susie looks at me.

"I don't think I've seen that one," I say.

The coke is starting to kick in.

"It's great," Susie continues. "The other kids start treating Jan like she *doesn't* have any brothers or sisters and, of course, she starts feeling lonely and left out."

"But then they ruin it by tagging on a happy ending," Wendy says. "Right?"

"Of *course,*" Susie says.

"Of course," Wendy says.

"Jan realizes she should feel *fortunate* for her family and everything," Susie says.

"I prefer game shows." Wendy turns away into the coffee room.

"Wendy's never going to be happy," Susie says, "until she can appreciate a good 'Brady Bunch.' "

Susie leads me into another room where art department people commit mysterious acts. She shows me a mock-up of *The T Team* poster: there are thirteen enormously overendowed girls gripping heavy firearms in the most phallic poses Susie's sex-obsessed mind can imagine. Artwork got the nod over photos because the actresses in *The T Team* look like used-up Playmates. Susie's renditions somehow all look like pubescent boy-crazy Catholic high school girls on the run from lesbian nuns.

"Is it horny enough?" Susie asks me. She's serious.

"A little subtle," I say, "but it works."

"Can you see the subliminals?"

I look closely. "No."

Susie gleefully shows me by running her finger over the words sex, fuck, cunt, and blow job generously etched all over everything just lightly enough to avoid being perceived by the conscious mind unless it knows what it's looking for. This is standard with advertising artwork, but Susie takes great pride in her excessiveness. She runs her fingers over disembodied penises coming up between the skirted girls' legs, small couples copulating on gun stocks, black death skulls drawn on breasts where nipples should be.

"And look at this," she says proudly.

She outlines a shadowy man bent over with an erection getting rear-ended by one of the pretty girls' guns.

"Genius," I say.

Susie grins.

△

Alone, I sit down and stare at the blue Selectric. I can't think of a line bad enough for *The T Team*.

The coke is making me want to do *something*, so I

start swiveling around in my chair. Around and around and around and around . . .

This is making me nauseous.

I stop swiveling before I black out and pick up last Sunday's L.A. *Times* and turn to the Calendar section because when I'm really hurting for ideas I look at other movie copy lines. It's depressing as hell but I'm desperate.

I find some stealable copy in a new Matt Dillon movie ad:

> *War Made Him a Man*
> *Love Made Him a Hero*

I try a variation on this for *The T Team:*

> *War Made Them Mad*
> *Love Made Them Crazy*

Not quite bad enough.

> *War Made Them Women*
> *Sex Made Them Crazy*

How can I write these things?

I study the ad for an alleged new comedy called *Vasectomy.*

> *Everything You Ever Wanted*
> *In a Marriage . . . and LESS!!!*

The three exclamation points amaze me.

I turn the page and encounter *The Men's Club.*

> *The Breakfast Club*
> *The Big Chill*
> And now
> *The Men's Club*
> Growing up is hard to do

Making semioriginal movies is harder still.

I can't think of a single movie that's comparable to *The T Team*. Thank God. Besides, the producer already solved that problem by ripping off the title from the "A Team."

Next page. An ad for *Crocodile Dundee*.

There's A Little Of Him In All Of Us

How Little? Six Inches?

I do not want Crocodile Dundee in me.

I put down the Calendar section and massage my temples. I don't know if this headache is coming from the coke, or the copy lines, or what, but it's coming.

I lie down on the floor and close my eyes and try to relax.

"Pain, pain, go away, come again some other day."

I try to think of good things. Good sensations.

Suddenly an idea comes to me and I get back up and type it down:

The T Team—This Is One Job They Can't Blow!

△

I skip lunch and take a nap in my office. After waking up I put on my sunglasses since the goddamn sun is shining right in my window, light a cigarette, and look over the copy lines thus far.

The blow-job line is far and away the best.

"God forgive me," I say.

My phone rings. I answer it and am relieved it's not God.

"I knew you were sleeping and didn't want to wake

21

you," says Angie, the receptionist. "Somebody called Y. J. Ogvassed called. He said he'll call again later."

"Thanks, Angie."

"Talk to you later, honey," she says and clicks me off to take some other call.

So somebody called Y. J. Ogvassed is in town. I type this out on the same paper as the *The T Team* copy. I like the look and sound of it and type it over and over again until I catch myself and wonder what the hell I'm doing.

I reach into my desk and pull out a postcard Y.J. sent from England. It's an old black and white photo of what appears to be a groom and his best men engaged in some strange physical activity. Black tie rugby, perhaps. The caption reads: "You construct intricate rituals that allow you to touch the skin of other men."

I derive my usual amount of amusement from this, and then put it back and return to staring at the bad copy lines.

Wendy and Susie enter without knocking and announce that I'm going out with them tonight to hear some friends of theirs play at the Anti-Club. I remind them I have a girlfriend who expects me.

"You can come willingly—" Wendy starts.

"—or you can make us make you." Susie finishes.

"Seriously," I say, "tonight's not a good night."

"Tonight could be a *very* good night," Susie says.

"No," I say, "I need to work some things out with Becky."

"Call her," Wendy says.

"These aren't the sorts of things you can work out on the phone."

"Call her and tell her you'll be home late," Wendy says.

"Very late," Susie adds.

"And you'll talk to her tomorrow or something."

"I appreciate the offer," I say.

"You can come with us willingly——" Wendy says.

"——or you can make us make you," Susie says.

"No, I really have to sort this out."

"If you *don't* come with us tonight, you'll be mad you didn't and you'll go home and blame it on her," Wendy says.

"Yeah," Susie says. "And you'll *beat* on her."

I roll my eyes.

"And," Susie says, "you'll accidentally *kill* her."

"And," Wendy says, "you'll be sent to jail."

"Where you'll be sodomized by hardened criminals."

"With AIDS."

I look at them and wonder what started this facetious tantrum. Some monstrous truth we're afraid to take too seriously. The usual.

"You're doing her a *favor* by coming with us," Wendy says.

"Right," Susie says.

Pause.

"An old friend of mine's in town," I say.

"*What?*"

"An old friend of mine's in town," I repeat. "I haven't seen him for a long time, and I don't know how to get a hold of him."

"What are you talking about?" Wendy says.

"He might be trying to get a hold of me," I explain.

"You can come with us willingly——" Wendy says.

"——or you can make us make you," they say in unison.

23

"You're coming with us tonight," Wendy says. "We're taking your convertible."

"Why," I ask.

"Because you're obviously angst-ridden about your twenty-fifth birthday," Wendy says.

I shake my head.

"Twenty-*five*." Susie laughs. "That's so *old*."

Susie is twenty-four.

"No," Wendy says, "you're not old until you're on the *wrong* side of twenty-five. Wait 'till *that* happens."

Wendy is twenty-six.

"I mean, why *my* car?" I say.

"Because," Wendy says and exits.

Then she pops her head back in. "Susie and I are planning on getting much too fucked up to drive." She closes my door.

Susie turns on my desk light and reads my copy for *The T Team* in the typewriter.

"Somebody called Y. J. Ogvassed's in town?"

"That's the old friend," I say, "not copy."

"Oh."

Susie makes a strange face, but she's the kind of girl who doesn't often ask about things not making sense because she expects that and she continues reading while I call my apartment and leave a message for Becky on the machine saying I'll be home late. Susie mouths "very late" in the background.

"The blow-job line is the best," Susie says loudly just before I can hang up the phone.

Δ

We drive down Melrose past the trendy stores. Wendy and Susie are drinking tall-boys and enjoying the convertible and I'm trying to remember what California law says about open containers in moving vehicles.

"Should you two be waving those beers around like Prom Queens on parade?" I say.

"Hand Zeke a Trident Sub," Wendy says.

Susie hands me a tall-boy and I think what the hell and start drinking. This is the first time I've ever been with Wendy and Susie outside the office and I can see I'm going to need every beer I can lay my hands on.

"This car is way cool," Susie says.

"*Rambler,*" Wendy notes.

"Rambler *American,*" I say.

"What year is it?" Wendy asks.

"Sixty-three."

"Way cool," Susie repeats. "It's like a *Ken and Barbie* car."

Wendy laughs. "And here's our own Ken doll," she nudges me and causes one hand to spill my beer and the other to lurch on the steering wheel and swerve the way cool car into the middle of the road. There are no cars coming the other way. I think this is fortunate as I move back into the right lane, then I wonder . . . and then wonder why the hell I'm wondering about that. . . .

"But Ken wouldn't drive a *black* car," Susie decides. "Ken would drive a *blue* car."

I could argue this point, but why? I just shrug.

"Your job tonight is to have fun," Wendy tells me. "We want *someone* to have fun."

"No angst allowed," Susie says.

I try to look like I'm having fun.

"*Ecstasy,*" Susie says. "We should get some ecstasy."

"Where," Wendy asks.

"There's this guy I sort of know in Silverlake."

"No," I say. "I'm not driving out to Silverlake."

"Well," Susie says, "let me think. Who around here can get us some ecstasy?"

"I'm not taking any ecstasy tonight," I say.

"Why not?" Susie says.

"Because," I say, "I don't deserve to feel that good."

We drive out of the trendy part of Melrose into an area with gang graffiti on the walls and scum in the street.

"What made you finally decide to come out with us," Wendy asks me.

"What do you mean?"

"We've practically tried to *kidnap* you before but you'd never come along."

"Well . . ." I say.

"We've got you now," Susie says.

Wendy does a mock-evil laugh.

"And you'll never be the same again," Susie says and starts humming the "Twilight Zone" theme.

Δ

We arrive and find a good parking spot. I wonder if this is a good omen.

At the front door a dozen or so people loiter, all appropriately attired for an every-night-is-Halloween dress code. Black leather and death icons seem the sartorial motif. I'm sure most clubs would consider these people undesirables. Wendy and Susie, of course, know them all.

I'm introduced to a few and then we go into the club and I realize why people are loitering outside—in here it's about six hundred degrees and crowded and noisy as hell.

The band on stage is playing very loud incoherent gloom-doom rock tunes. ". . . *all we ever wanted was everything, all we ever got was shit and peanut butter sandwiches . . .*" or something like that.

I excuse myself to go to the bathroom, join the line, and finally get into this filthy dark closet with a toilet. I read the wall while I urinate.

Written over all else in big orange letters:

"I DON'T CARE ABOUT YOU. FUCK YOU!"
—Fear

Underneath in pencil:

if the god damn rolling stones had any self respect they would hurry up and die

And:

MTV is for retards

And:

Whatever happened to Shaun Cassidy?

Someone's answer:

It's Hare Krishna Time

I doubt this but I wonder?

I shake and zip up and, as I step out, two guys who are dressed like extras for a Penelope Spherris movie look me over. One says, "Do enough coke, Biff?"

I walk on like I don't hear and find Wendy and Susie at the bar. I buy three beers while Wendy and Susie look around and say hi to people. It dawns on me that Wendy and Susie must lead strange lives outside Big Gun because they seem very much a part of whatever cliques

27

come here. Wendy says something I can't hear over the loud gloomy music.

"What?" I say.

"Are you having fun?" Wendy says loudly.

"I'm amused."

"We want you to have fun," Susie yells in my ear.

"I'll try," I yell back.

"What?" Wendy yells.

"I told Susie I would try to have fun," I yell to Wendy.

"Good."

Pause.

"Do you see any men you think we should meet?" Susie yells at me.

"What?" Wendy says and leans her head in.

"I asked him if he could see any men we should meet."

Wendy looks at me.

"You're the ones who know people here," I point out.

"We need to meet somebody *new*," Wendy yells.

"The guys we know . . ." Susie shakes her head.

"They're mutts," Wendy yells.

I look around. I can see her point.

"You have to help us meet somebody *new*," Wendy yells.

"Somebody totally *new and improved*," Susie yells, and they both laugh.

"Well," I say, "this is certainly a great place to meet someone. To talk and really get to know a person."

"What?" This time in unison.

"Nothing," I yell. "I was joking."

"What?" Susie yells, "What's the joke?"

28

"Never mind," I yell.

We drink more beers that I pay for and the band their friends are in, The Bleeding Sirens, finally come out and we jockey for space near the stage and get close enough to the speakers that I soon feel numbed by the sound. They play pop/cowpunk music with lyrics that sound like they were borrowed from Jack Kerouac.

I'm interested.

I'm particularly interested in the lead singer—a young trampy girl with bleached blond hair wearing shredded Levis and a cowgirl blouse and long black lace gloves. She somehow looks like a young Jessica Lange. But with Marilyn Monroe's breasts and cat-eye glasses.

I think I establish eye contact. But making people think they've established that is part of her job, so I just try to enjoy the show. Make it worth suffering permanent hearing damage.

But afterward I'm in a back room of the club with Wendy and Susie, an actress whose mother owns the place, the band and some hangers-on, and the Jessica Lange look-a-like singer is flirting with me. I wonder why. Maybe because I'm the only guy in the room without an earring or a tattoo. She probably thinks I'm strange.

When the drummer says it would be cool if we all went with the band to a party at this house on famed Blue Jay Way, the singer looks at me. "You got a car," she asks.

"Yes," I say.

"Can I come with you?"

"Sure."

Wendy and Susie smirk at me.

△

The house is ten million dollars' worth of tacky.

It's loaded with bounteous amounts of drugs and booze and hangers-on and sleazy rich men buying whatever they can get.

Wendy and Susie are talking with a group of guys about their own age. Wendy looks bored and Susie looks drunk. Younger girls around them are weighing bids from the older men.

The singer and I grab a couple beers from the refrigerator and wander around the house until we find a deck that looks out over the city.

I developed some rapport with the singer in the ride here by playing The Replacements' "Let It Be," and now I tell her I thought I recognized some Kerouac references in her lyrics.

"Who?" she says.

"He's a writer," I say. "A dead writer. The Beat Generation."

She nods.

"He wrote *On the Road*," I continue, "and some other books."

"Oh, yeah."

Pause.

"You're not from L.A., are you?" she says.

"No."

"You sort of look like Sam Shepard," she says, "except your teeth are good."

I'm not sure how to respond to this. She might be joking—but her smile is sexual, not humorous. I hope she's joking.

"*Really,*" she says.

"It's strange," I say, like *I* might be joking, "but when I first saw you I thought you sort of looked like Jessica Lange."

30

"Yeah?"

"Yes."

She buys it. I find our mutually misguided attraction sick and sad and amusing, and wonder why she seems pleased.

She pulls out a joint and I light it for her, but when she passes it to me I decline and stick with my cigarette.

"You don't smoke dope?"

"No."

"Why not?"

I shrug.

"It's cool," she says and smokes on.

"I have enough strange shit in my head as it is," I suddenly say.

She nods knowingly. At least I think it's knowingly. It bothers me that I can't tell what kind of nod she has. I know Becky's nods. At least most of the time.

As I look out at the smoggy glow of the city lights and the singer smokes the joint in silence, I start wondering if maybe I should call Becky. But watching the singer smoke I think about how goddamn sexy and special and potent she seemed on stage and how I wanted to fuck her.

She catches me looking at her. She exhales a long toke and says, "I like it for sex."

I nod.

△

We find the weight-lifting room and shove a couple barbells up against the door and turn out the lights so there's only the glow of the city coming through the window glimmering off the exercise/torture equipment.

She starts stripping in front of a mirror.

31

Though she's conscious of my reaction, she's watching herself as the jeans alone take what seems like almost a minute to squiggle out of. She admires her body's reflection as she stands there in her black panties, and I notice the panties have a little rip in the ass.

She rolls her panties down the unshaven yet almost hairless legs. No tan line. The t-shirt comes off next in a fast gesture that makes her breasts bob.

Then she turns and comes to me. She's still wearing the long black lace gloves. The gloves reach out and start unbuttoning my oxford. The oxford comes off. She kneels down. She deftly undoes my belt. Unbuttons the khakis. Even knows to undo the French flap. Then the sound of that zipper. The gloves have it. The pants are wrapped around the ankles. She crawls around behind. She rests her face against my hip and looks in the mirror. I look in the mirror. The gloves come around front and the boxers, too, are brought down to the ankles.

I feel a teenage-strength hard-on building.

And I know I should have a Trojan with me, but I also know I probably wouldn't use it if I did.

She comes back around to the front and stands up about a foot away from me. I can feel her body. Neither of us moves. We can hear each other breathing, we can smell each other. The animal senses are rousing from a primal slumber. She puts the black lace gloved hands on my chest and I almost suffer a goddamn cardiac arrest. Still, I don't move.

She opens her mouth. "I suppose I should tell you," she says, "that I have herpes."

△

In the familiar smog-blue light before sunrise, I'm

driving Wendy and Susie down Hollywood Boulevard as the litter blows along the street.

"Then she asks, Is that a problem?" I relate.

"What did you say?" Susie finds this terrifically funny.

"I said, Fuck yes it's a problem."

"Another sad Hollywood-relationship story," Wendy says. "We'll read about it in the L.A. Dee Da column."

I'm starting to laugh. "Then she says, You mean you *don't* have it?"

Susie laughs.

"Call me old-fashioned," I say.

△

We arrive at Susie's small studio apartment, not far from Big Gun, and it's decided we'll hang out here with Susie's dirty clothes and dirty dishes and drink coffee for the three hours we have until it's time to hit the office.

"Why do guys who seem to have brains go for bimbos," Wendy asks me over coffee.

I start to say something—

"Because they're fucked up," Wendy says.

"It's true," Susie says.

"Men are really intimidated by women with brains." Wendy is facing me. "Why?"

I start to say something—

"Because they're fucked up," Wendy says.

"Men don't want to just *talk* to a girl," Susie says. "What do men *want?*"

I start to say something—

"Men are fucked up," Wendy says.

"And it's not just *men,*" Susie says.

33

"*Every*body's fucked up," Wendy says.

"But we don't mean you, Zeke," Susie adds. "You're the normalest person we know."

△

I sip on Susie's awful coffee and smoke a cigarette and thumb through the sticky pages of an old *Art Dog* magazine, publishing home to some of Susie's poetry as it turns out:

> sometimes i see stars
> and think of eternity and mortality
> sometimes i see stars
> and think of the starship enterprise

Plus there's a photo of Susie. She's holding a "lifelike" rubber dildo while mounting a children's rocking horse and she's wearing black leather shorts only and there's blood dripping from her eyes. It's a good shot.

"I'm a bright person and I can't understand why men and everything are so fucked up," Wendy says.

Suddenly I remember this lame line I overheard at the party. "It's the eighties."

We're punchy and delirious from the booze and the drugs and the hours, and this stunningly stupid summary on my part sadly amuses us.

We laugh for a while until we realize there's really nothing to laugh about.

Suddenly I'm exhausted. The coffee seems to have a reverse effect on me, the way uppers did when I was a curiously hyper kid, so I decide to lie down on Susie's bed—a queen-size mattress on the floor that doubles as a wastebasket for wadded-up paper and God knows what else.

I feel myself falling asleep.

But I sort of wake up as my pants are being taken off and think, Oh, how nice of somebody to think of taking my clothes off, but I wake up a little further and realize there are naked female bodies on either side and it's not a dream.

We have desperate sweaty sex without any actual fucking, which is probably my drunken fault, and then we shower separately and I go out to my car alone and find somebody has scratched with a key or something across one whole side panel.

I start to laugh, but the laughing becomes coughing.

△

"Well, you didn't get up this morning because you didn't go to bed, you've been watching the whites of your eyes turn red . . ." It could be the Big Gun elevator muzak, or it could be my head. *Must* be my head.

I step out of the elevator and I'm bushwhacked.

"Zeke!" A friendly scream, I think, but one can't be too sure in this town.

"No," I say. "I'm afraid you're mistaken."

The face chuckles. "Zeke, you look great. How the hell are you?"

I remember: Chris something. We took some of the same cinema classes at U.S.C. I'm in no mood to talk old times or share Hollywood horror stories, but he's a good guy and I want to behave better than I feel.

My mother gave me some advice I wonder about but try to follow anyway: act polite and nobody will notice you're crazy. My mother is polite and everybody notices she's crazy.

35

"Fine, thanks," I say. "'How are you, Chris?"

"Great," Chris says.

"Good," I say. "Excuse me, but I'm considerably later than usual and I have to get to my office."

"You *work* here?"

"If you mean am I *employed* here, yes."

"What do you do?"

"I write bad copy for bad movies." The stock answer.

"You?"

"No, my evil twin brother Mark."

Chris chuckles. "Of all people, I thought you'd be working regular by now. I mean, like selling scripts or directing or something."

"Well . . ."

"What happened?"

"What happened?"

"I mean, what have you been doing," he asks. "Like that excellent script you wrote after Boyle's class? Didn't somebody option it?"

"Yes."

"What happened?"

"Nothing."

"I guess it was probably too visual."

I light a cigarette.

"Haven't you kept on writing? You were a great writer."

"Thank you." I wonder why he's using the past tense.

"You should—"

"Excuse me," I say, "but I really should get to my office before lunch."

"I just sold a script here," Chris blurts out.

"Congratulations."

36

"It's the third I've sold."

"Congratulations."

"Maybe you'll write the copy for it."

"Maybe."

"It's about a lone-wolf kind of guy who goes into an unnamed Latin American country to rescue some buddies being held prisoner by drug dealers. He has this robot that helps him."

I can't tell if he's joking. "Congratulations," I say.

"This town ain't so tough."

"No."

"I know you're going to have a lot of success, too," Chris assures me. "You're . . . you *look* like a good writer."

"Interesting concept."

Chris laughs. "You've got that *aura*," he says.

"I've gotta go, Chris."

"Let's get together sometime."

"Maybe I'll see you around here," I suggest.

"No," he says, "I probably won't be around here much. They just told me today they're bringing in somebody else to rewrite my script."

He's not joking, and I suddenly feel for the guy. "Sorry to hear that," I say.

"I don't care."

I shrug, thinking he must care. He probably cares too much to talk about it.

"I really don't give a shit," he says.

I look at him. He means it.

"You learn not to give a shit," he tells me.

I don't want to learn not to give a shit. But I just nod and politely say "good-bye" before I'm trapped into making lunch plans with him.

I lock my office door and unplug the phone and light another cigarette. I have three messages on my desk:

Becky called. Y. J. Ogvassed called again. And Peg wants to see me. Unlike other Big Gun employees, I actually get along with Peg. But right now I can't cope.

There's a knock on the door. Oh, shit. The door-knob is rattling. Thank God it's locked. More knocking. I stand up and move away from it.

This is fucking ridiculous.

I open the door. It's Wendy and Susie, all smiles and giggles. No embarrassment or guilt or shame. I have a lot to learn from these two.

"We just wanted to tell you to beware of Peg," Wendy says. "She's in an especially bitchy mood today."

"And we wanted to see how you were," Susie says, smiling.

"I'm fine," I say. "Considering."

They giggle some more and say they've got to get back to the art department in case Peg checks in, then they exit with winks and waves.

The phone rings. I freeze. It continues ringing. I stare at it for a few rings more. It won't stop ringing . . . so I walk out the door.

"Tell anyone who cares I became violently ill," I say as I walk out past Angie's desk.

"Sure, honey," she says, and when she wishes me a good weekend I realize it's Friday.

The elevator doors open and I step in just as Peg steps out.

"Where are *you* going?" she says.

"To hell," I say. "Maybe I'll see you there."

Before either of us can figure out why the fuck I've said this the elevator doors close and I'm gone.

△

I drive down Sunset. Somehow the billboards are more aggravating than usual, something sicker being sold, and somehow it has something to do with Becky and me.

The Plague.

I look away and turn up KROQ. You should always be able to depend on loud music for salvation.

But I have to stop for a red light right under the worst billboard in world history. Sylvester Stallone is standing above the street with a wooden match in his mouth, a wooden expression on his face, and a gun with a glowing red tip in his dirty black-gloved hands. CRIME IS THE DISEASE. MEET THE CURE. NOW OUT ON VIDEO.

Meet me as I puke.

The saddest thing is that this is my job.

I turn up the radio loud enough to make a less experienced rock aficionado's ears bleed.

After driving aimlessly around the L.A. freeway system for a while, I start to feel like I'm living in a Joan Didion novel. *That* scares me enough to send me home.

△

I pull into the parking lot beside Becky's white MG. I walk past a man with a shopping cart going through the garbage, and just as I'm coming to my building door I'm cut off by John, one of the many local street kids. He asks if I want any pot.

"No," I say.

"Some ludes?"

"No, thanks."

"Speed?"

"Nope."

"Coke?"

39

"Not today."

"Why not?"

I shrug. He looks around.

"Smack?" he says. "You know anyone needs some smack?"

"No," I say. "Afraid not."

"If you ever do, let me know," he says. "I'm around."

"Okay."

"You sure you don't need anything?"

"No," I say. "Not right now."

"You *look* like you do," he says, and laughs once as he rides back into the crowd on his skateboard.

I start to open the door to the building, then realize there's no way I can face Becky now. "You can run but you can't hide." I wonder who first said this as I walk back to my car.

△

The radio isn't playing what I want to hear so I put on an old Elvis Costello tape. *"As I walk thru this wicked world, looking for light in the darkness of insanity . . ."*

I drive up Pacific Avenue and get on the Santa Monica Freeway at 4th Street. Headed east, I can feel the air grow thicker and hotter and generally uglier as I approach downtown.

I decide to turn off south on the Harbor Freeway. This takes me past Watts. My only images of Watts come from old news footage of the '65 riots. I doubt it's any better in there today. Probably worse.

On the San Diego Freeway south the air starts to get cooler and better. I'm glad for my convertible as I cruise past green signs telling when to turn for places like Manhattan Beach and Newport Beach.

Eventually I pull over at a bluff. I get out of the car and walk to the edge. I step over the guard rail and look down at the waves breaking on the rocks. I throw a stone over. It disappears from my vision before it's halfway down. I wonder how long a body would take to fall, wonder what the body would look like *after* the fall.

As I stare down at the surf I suddenly realize I'm hungry, so I get back in the car and drive off in search of food.

△

I find a casual seaside restaurant, almost empty between lunch and dinner.

At the bar, prepared to kill time with a newspaper, I order a J&B neat. The bartender gives me a good drink and I give him a good tip. I feel we've established a good working relationship.

The Scotch tastes warm. I light a cigarette.

After my second Scotch and third cigarette, I feel sufficiently anesthetized to open up the paper. I skim the usual front-page items: violence, starvation, sex murders, neo-Nazis training for Armageddon, bombings and wars and protests and legal and illegal arms sales and a woman with quintuplets.

I do read one interesting article. A follow-up story about the mailman who arrived on the job one day armed with a couple .45's and started slaughtering his co-workers. The reporter tries to make some sense of this by interviewing friends of the man, psychiatrists, jaded cops, and so on. His article succeeds only in emphasizing everyone's pagan confusion.

But there is one wonderful image: someone remembers the mailman riding around on a bicycle built for two—by himself.

I wonder why anyone is surprised he snapped.

Then I read the review of a new Spielberg movie that Spielberg neither wrote or directed, and scan the ads for new movies. If anything, this is as depressing as the front page.

I try for sports. Another athlete OD'd on cocaine. I skip to the back pages. Tires and guns are for sale.

I decide to find a phone and call a friend. Standing at the phone trying to decide who to call, I realize I don't have any real close friends in this town. I have many acquaintances, none of whom I wish to talk to.

And I don't know what I can say to Becky.

I settle for an old buddy from Saint Luke school days who, if not a blood brother, is intelligent and amusing and likes to drink. He agrees to meet me for dinner in Newport Beach.

I hate to leave this bar, having established such a good relationship with the bartender, but life is hard. I leave the newspaper behind for the next guy.

△

"Money's the answer," Bob says as he dips a crab leg into melted butter. "Shitloads of it."

I hold a forkful of veal in my left hand and a cigarette in my right.

"Did you ever think it'd be like this?" I say. "When you were a kid, reading classics like *The Grinch Who Stole Christmas,* did you ever imagine how ugly it was out here?"

Bob shakes his head and washes down his crab with a gin and tonic.

"Nobody told *me,*" I say.

"No," he says. "No kid would ever believe it."

We both laugh.

"I don't know," I say.

"It's the *economy.*" Bob looks up at me, empty-handed. "In the sixties it was different, those freaks knew all they had to do was cut their hair and take a bath and stay off acid for a week and they could step right into a managerial position at IBM. It's not like that anymore. The economy's changed."

I nod.

"We don't have *time* for orgies and acid, listening to *Rubber Soul* for sixteen hours straight."

I sort of laugh.

"We have to *compete,*" he says, reaching back to the crabmeat.

I put down my fork and reach for the wine glass.

"The only answer is to make so much goddamn money they can't touch you," Bob says.

"Then what?"

"Make your own reality," he says. "*Buy* it."

I frown as Bob laughs at himself.

△

After dinner we're standing in the parking lot, and I tell him I've been having troubles with Becky.

"Is *that* why you were so miserable at your birthday party?"

"I guess so."

"We thought maybe you were freaked about getting old."

43

"No."

"So you're having troubles with Becky, huh? She *looks* great."

"I know."

Pause.

"What kind of troubles," Bob asks.

"I don't know," I say. "If I knew I'd probably know what to do."

"*I* know what to do."

"I'm listening."

"Get laid," he says.

"Sex is *not* the problem," I say. "It's the only thing left."

"No," he says, "I mean with someone *else*. Hide the salami with someone new."

"I have."

"Who?"

"A couple girls."

"A *couple?*"

I don't want to explain, so I just nod.

"How'd you feel about it," Bob asks.

"How'd I feel?"

"If you *liked* it, you don't love Becky," he advises. "If you *didn't* like it, you do love Becky. If you didn't like it *and* you feel guilty, you're pussy whipped."

"I don't know," I say. I can't remember the last time I heard the expression *pussy whipped*.

"Then we'll just have to go out and do it again tonight," Bob says, smiling. "Just like old times."

I realize it's a sign of how far gone I am that I don't even argue.

△

We're driving in Bob's gray BMW to a bar where

he thinks we can get laid when a beer commercial comes on promising we can have it all.

"It's part of the Plague," I say. "This ad."

"What?"

"I hate hearing this shit," I say, turning off the radio.

Bob shrugs and reaches over and pushes in a cassette, early Springsteen. The Boss is singing about the lonely and who he loves only and having faith and about a girl. A girl who isn't beautiful but is all right with him.

I'm getting into the music but Bob starts laughing and says to me, "The Boss married an AMW."

"An AMW?"

"Actress-Model-Waitress."

That about ruins it all.

△

The beachy bar features a lot of tan young healthy bodies and bad top-forty music. "Whenever I come into places like these," Bob says, "I always think I could slaughter everybody in here with an Uzi and the world wouldn't miss a thing."

"You want to leave?" I ask.

"No, I want to get laid."

I order a Scotch at the bar, Bob a gin and tonic. We look around. There are a lot of very pretty girls and a lot of very pretty boys and a very sad air of desperation and boredom.

"Doesn't look promising," Bob says.

"Fire up some scintillating conversation with somebody," I suggest.

"These girls don't want to hear about anything except your Porsche and cocaine."

I light a cigarette.

"I never get laid at places like this," Bob says.

"Then what are we doing here?"

"*Rarely* do I get laid at places like this," he corrects himself.

"You want to go?"

"No, I want to get laid."

Bob kills his drink and works on attracting the bartender's attention for another.

I look around and notice that there's not a single girl here I want to make an effort for. I wonder if it's me or them.

Bob gets two drinks for himself, and we wander into the human morass and the air seems hot and smoky and I suddenly feel nauseous. I want to get out.

But I see a tall gorgeous blonde, twenty-one at the oldest, who appears to feel the way I do. She's wearing an oversized men's Brooks Brothers shirt, peach colored and buttoned down, old Levis and scruffy penny loafers without socks, and she's almost six feet tall. She could be a model—or as they're now known, a module—but I'm not going to ask.

I watch her blow off a series of guys.

Bob is watching me watch her. "Looks good, big guy," he says.

Normally I would not go up and talk to this girl, but right now I'm not feeling normal and I've got nothing to lose. I go up to her. "What are you doing here?" I say.

She looks at me. "I wish I knew."

"Let me know if you find an answer."

This is starting to feel awkward, and I'm about to move on but she says, "What are *you* doing here?"

"I'm here with a friend who came to get laid."

She smiles. "So am I."

I nod. We smile at each other. I wonder why.

"My friend's over there, being slowly bored to death by a surfer," she says. "Where's yours?"

"Leering at you."

I point Bob out to her. At first he pretends not to be watching us, but when she signals for him to come join us, he starts making his way over.

"I'm Kelly," she says to me.

"Zeke."

We shake hands and Bob joins us.

"Kelly," I say, "this is Bob Cutler."

They shake hands.

"I understand you're here to find a bedwarmer," Kelly says.

Bob laughs. "Well," he says, "I'm sure as shit not here for intellectual stimulation."

I suddenly realize he's drunk.

"You and my friend Cathy will get along fabulously," Kelly says.

Bob looks around. "Where is she?"

"Coming over right now."

A short, bleached blonde joins us and introductions are made, and she and Bob seem to find each other acceptable.

"You from back East," Cathy asks me. "Like Kelly?"

"No," I say. "Seattle."

"I hear it rains a lot there," Cathy says.

"It does."

"Really?"

"All the time," I say. "Great suicide weather."

Pause.

"Seattle has a very high suicide rate," I say.

Bob looks at me like he's been poleaxed.

"But *personally*," I say, "I think sunshine can be as depressing as rain. Much more so, in fact."

"Zeke went to U.S.C.," Bob blurts out.

"Oh," Cathy says.

I look at Kelly, who's smiling. "Let's get out of here," she says.

"Excellent idea," Bob says.

"We can go back to my place," Kelly says.

All apparently think this is an improvement on listening to me talk about suicide.

Cathy goes with Bob. I ride with Kelly in her car—a convertible Mercedes, no less—and offer drunken repartee that seems to amuse her. She bounces back just enough banter to keep me from lapsing into a monologue.

She *looks* lethal at the wheel. She's wearing sunglasses to keep her hair from blowing into her eyes and every time we pass a streetlight I feel like a photo has been snapped for next month's *Vogue*.

I babble all the way to her beach house.

△

We're standing on the deck, the four of us, drinking and looking out at the moonlight in the clouds and I'm feeling strangely close to Kelly. The waves are breaking about thirty yards away.

The Scotch keeps me warm. It also keeps me from thinking too hard about Becky.

"Excellent real estate," Bob says. "Your parents?"

"My husband's," Kelly answers.

I drain my glass. "Anybody else need a refill," I ask.

"Yes, please," Kelly says.

"No, thanks," Cathy says.

"I'll come with you," Bob volunteers.

"No," I say, "I've got it."

"Okay." Bob hands me his glass.

After mixing the drinks, I snoop around to establish whether the husband still lives here. Looks to me like he does. And I remember the size of the shirt Kelly's wearing. He's a large man.

By the time I come back out with the drinks, attention has moved from the big body of salt water to the smaller body of chlorine water right here on the deck.

"Anybody feel like taking a hot tub," Kelly asks.

"Good idea," Cathy says.

"Yeah," Bob says enthusiastically. "Sounds great."

"Come on," Cathy says, "let's get some towels."

Cathy leads Bob into the house. Kelly and I stay.

"Strong drink," Kelly says.

I nod.

"You want to go in," she asks. "The hot tub?"

"Will your husband be joining us when he gets home?"

"No."

"Will he be getting home?" I ask. "I mean, not that we're doing anything we shouldn't be doing but your husband, for all I know, is a paranoid who carries dangerous firearms."

"He's out of town for three weeks."

I think for a moment. "How old is your husband?"

"Thirty-six."

"How old are you?"

"Nineteen."

I nod.

"Any more questions," she asks.

"Yes," I say, "what the hell am I doing here?"

"You're here because I want you here."

"Why?"

"You strike me as interesting," she says.

"Oh?"

"And I need that, because I'm bored out of my mind most of the time."

I understand and appreciate her answer, but I still don't know what I'm doing here.

"Any more questions?" she says again.

I shake my head.

"Then come on," she says, "we'll get towels."

She takes my hand and I follow. I can feel the inevitability of sex. A mixed feeling.

While she's in her bathroom picking out towels, I'm in the bedroom staring in awe at her three enormous closets of clothes.

She comes out and sees me. "Ridiculous, isn't it?" she says.

I nod.

"It's because of you," she says.

"Pardon me?"

"Men," she says. "You make us dress for you. You should see some of the ads I've had to do."

I wish she hadn't admitted her profession.

"They're all geared to selling things men find alluring," she says.

"And you're party to this."

"Yes," she says, "but I'm well paid."

"Oh, then it's okay."

"Seriously," she says, "I think about these things. But I figure that's the way it is. Women have been adorning themselves for centuries, it's this ritualistic thing . . ."

A sociological treatise from a module.

△

We're all in the hot tub. Bob and Cathy and Kelly are passing a bottle of mineral water. I'm drinking Scotch.

Kelly says they're studying Sartre's *No Exit* in her acting class.

"Have you ever read it," she asks me.

I nod.

"What did you think?"

"Sartre and Camus were just two guys who couldn't get laid," I say. "They weren't particularly good looking and they weren't rich, so they figured they had to become celebrity philosophers."

Bob and Kelly laugh, but then Bob looks at Cathy and realizes she doesn't get it.

"Seen any good movies lately?" Bob says to Cathy.

I laugh because I think he's joking. But he isn't joking, and soon enough he and Cathy are well into the latest John Hughes movie.

Kelly winks at me and one of her hands goes underwater. The hand grabs my knee, then slides up and starts massaging my thigh. This feels surprisingly good and I wish she'd do the other thigh as well.

But instead her hand goes where she thinks I want it to be.

I try to tune out Bob and Cathy and close my eyes and try to concentrate on appreciating the idyllic situation I'm in . . . Kelly . . . moon . . . ocean . . . warm water on my body . . . warm Scotch in my body . . . the hand job . . .

It feels like a scene from a movie or a what-sort-of-man reads *Playboy* ad, not real. No wonder I feel numb.

I need a new movie.

△

I'm in a dark room in a strange bed with a truly spectacular strapping body and trying to tell her I don't feel like fucking.

"You're afraid of diseases?" she says.

"Yes, but that's not the problem."

She looks at me.

"Do you want me to say something awful like, 'It's me, not you,' " I ask.

She shakes her head. Then says, "Can we at least cuddle?"

We cuddle and that much feels okay.

△

When we get up the next morning I want to ask Bob how my behavior fits into his theory of human relationships, but he's gone.

Cathy and Kelly talk for a while, then Cathy leaves and Kelly and I have strawberries, cream, and champagne on the deck. It's a good brunch.

I'm glad I have my sunglasses with me.

△

She drives me to the parking lot where I left my car and I'm surprised to find it hasn't been towed.

"I'd like to see you again sometime," she says.

I'm looking at my car—really pleased it wasn't towed.

"Can I call you," she asks.

"Do you really want to?"

Pause.

We kiss each other quickly and both drive away.

I put U2 into the cassette deck. *"And we can break through, though torn in two we can be one, I will begin again, I will begin again . . ."* and I'm thinking about how when I was younger and more religious I felt everything in my life happened for a reason.

△

Back home, I unlock the door and Becky is lying on the trashed oriental rug wearing my robe and studying her script of *Waiting for Godot*.

I wonder how Jean Paul and Albert and Sam would feel if they knew how popular they've become.

"Good morning," I say.

She doesn't look up. I know immediately this is going to be even worse than I'd expected.

The apartment is a big hardwood floor rectangle that contains the kitchen, my desk, the computer, the VCR and TV, a turntable and tape deck and CD player and speakers, bar stools, and the futon, all in one space. Windows in the raw brick wall look west over the ocean. A small bedroom is on the north side, a small bathroom on the south. To get out of Becky's sight, I must retire to one of these rooms. No, I think. Face the music, Zeke.

"How are rehearsals going?" I say.

She doesn't look up.

"You and Miss TV Star getting along?"

No response.

"They're filming the play for cable, right?"

Nada.

"Sorry."

Still she doesn't look up.

"Not about the filming for cable," I say. "I mean I'm sorry about my . . . you know."

Zip.

"You want to talk about it?"

Zero.

"Or would you rather just simmer?"

Squat.

"Okay," I say, "as long you're simmering because you *want* to."

She turns a page.

"I was talking to this producer today," I say, "and I told him you were in a female-cast version of *Waiting for Godot* and he said that was like doing a homosexual *Jesus Christ Superstar.*" This is a lie, of course, calculated to piss her off and provoke a response.

No response.

I think if she's just *acting* like she's hurt, it's a convincing performance. But I catch myself and realize *of course* she's really hurt.

But I don't know what to do about it.

I walk over to the refrigerator for lunch—a Corona with a slice of lime, and I notice an almost empty wine bottle next to her tofu burgers and I remember at least two or three bottles were in here a couple days ago. I look over at her. There's an empty glass by one of her bare feet.

"Been drinking a bit, have we?" I say.

I think she smiles a teeny smile, but maybe not. I come over and sit down on the rug. "What the hell is wrong," I ask. "And I don't mean about last night. I know *that's* wrong. I mean what's *been* wrong?"

No response.

"I thought you wanted to talk."

No response.

"I want to talk. I want to work this out." Did I actually say that?

No response.

I drink the rest of my lunch, and go into the bedroom and lie down without taking off anything but my shoes.

I lie with my eyes closed and I lie with my eyes open.

I know I'm not going to be able to fall asleep. My throat hurts, my head throbs, my muscles ache. And I'm afraid my body and mind have moved beyond the range of natural biological repair work.

I stand up and look out the window at the beautiful day. A street musician on the boardwalk is doing a raspy cover version of "Blowin' in the Wind." Above him two tall palm trees are waving slightly in the offshore ocean breeze and the sun is at a perfect three-o'clock angle that sparkles on the breaking waves and a large sailboat is beating against the wind.

I'm staring for who knows how long when I'm distracted by something on the boardwalk below. Right next to our local Dylan two men are exchanging very loud obscenities.

"Fuck you!"

"Fuck *you*."

"You'd like to, wouldn't you, faggot?"

These are grown men. One is a professional Venice bum complete with Ratso Rizzo overcoat for the seventy-degree chill, hoisting a quart of beer. The other is hopping around a lot and his pant leg is waving in the wind and I realize he has only one leg. His crutches are about twenty feet behind him on a bench.

55

The musician quits playing to watch, and his audience also focuses in on the potential violence.

Suddenly, realizing he's attracted everyone's attention, the one-legged man lashes out with a quick right and catches the bum square in the nose. Slightly staggered, the bum backs off. One-Leg shouts a few more obscenities, spits, and returns to the bench and sits next to his crutches.

The musician resumes playing. *"How many years must some people exist . . ."* The crowd turns back to the music.

But I watch the bum, who slinks away to a corner of a building and feels his bloody nose. He lies down and pulls on his bottle.

After emptying the bottle, the bum walks over to the one-legged man and they start talking. I wish I could hear what they're saying.

The musician can hear. He looks over as he continues singing. His crowd also looks over. The one-legged man then shouts, "Don't ever fucking kick my crutches again, man."

I can't hear the bum's response.

"I'll be your friend, man," the one-legged man shouts. "But don't *ever* fucking kick my crutches."

The bum says something. The musician stops playing.

"I don't care if I *was* an asshole," the one-legged man continues shouting. "Don't ever *fucking* kick my crutches." Then he hops up and swings a crazed right but the bum stumbles out of the fist's path and One-Leg goes sprawling off balance onto the cement. He hops right back up. The bum gives him plenty of space. Both start shouting at the same time.

Keep singing, Mr. Musician, I say to myself. I think if he keeps singing everything will be okay.

But the musician and his crowd are riveted. Even I find myself thinking this could be a potentially interesting fight. This is sickening.

The bum looks at everybody looking at him, then shakes his head and walks away. The one-legged man curses the bum's back, spits, and returns to his crutches on the bench.

The musician starts singing again and the crowd's attention follows. I look out at the palm trees and the sun and the ocean and the sailboat and listen to the music, *"How many times must a man turn his head and pretend . . ."* but then it stops.

I look down. This bum, either a persistent peace-maker or a masochist, is approaching the one-legged man yet again.

Keep singing, Mr. Musician.

But the musician and his crowd and everybody else are more interested in seeing what comes next.

I turn and go back into the main room where Becky is just sitting and staring at her hands. I sit down next to her. She still won't look at me, but I can see her eyes and they're red.

"Want to talk," I ask.

She studies her hands.

"I'll talk," I say. "I'll just pretend I'm in a confessional. Your part, when I'm finished, is to tell me to do twenty thousand Hail Marys. Okay?"

No response.

"Well," I say, and then try to get it all out in one breath: "I had a worse than usually awful day at the office and then I went to a club with Susie and Wendy to see this

57

band they know and the lead singer who I found attractive
in a sick fantasy-image kind of way was flirting with me
after the show and so I drove her to this party on Blue Jay
Way and we went into this exercise room and were about
to fuck but she had herpes and told me thank God so I
split with Wendy and Susie and went to Susie's place and
we were all delirious and I fell asleep but I woke up and I
was sort of having sex with both of them and then I went
to the office but I couldn't take it so I left and went driving
and I don't know what I was looking for but I wound up in
San Clemente and then Newport where I had dinner with
Bob Cutler and then we went to this beachy bar and met
these girls and went back to this girl's husband's beach
house and sat around drunk in a hot tub and though there
was a lot of horseplay I was too tired or numb or drunk or
disgusted to fuck so I went to sleep and when I got up she
took me to my car and I came home."

"*What?*"

"We're talking now?"

"What did you say?"

"I cheated the last couple nights."

"Yes," she says, "I heard *that*."

"Then why did you say 'what'?"

"I want to know what you just said."

"I just said I cheated. Triple cheated if you think of
a three-way as a double."

"What did you say about herpes?"

"I didn't get it. I didn't sleep with that one. I slept
with Wendy and Susie."

Pause.

"Why," she asks.

"I don't know."

"Did you use a condom?"

"No, but Wendy and Susie don't have anything."

"How do you *know?*"

"They're both paranoid," I say. "They get tested monthly."

Becky stares at me.

"There's something here I should point out," I say. "There was no actual fucking."

"Then what did you do?"

"Just fucked around."

Pause.

"Did you enjoy it," she asks.

"I've had worse times."

"Fine."

"Just kidding."

"I'm supposed to ask questions like that," she says. "Right?"

"What?"

"You did it so I could ask these questions and you could explain yourself, right?"

"Wrong."

"Then why?"

"I don't know."

"Is there something about the gutter that appeals to you?"

"We are all of us in the gutter, but some of us are looking at the stars," I say with the necessary facetiousness.

"Oscar Wilde," she answers correctly.

"We are all of us in the gutter, but some of us are looking at the slime."

"A jerk," she answers correctly.

I nod.

"Now what?" she says.

"Get out the gun and shoot me."

"I'm afraid of that gun."

"Mace me."

"No."

"Maim me?"

"No."

"Tie me up and whip me with silk ties?"

"Maybe." She smiles and I feel a lot better.

But suddenly she's crying, which makes me desperately uneasy, and then we're holding onto each other and kissing as she cries.

Next thing I know we're having sex, which seems more sensible to me than crying, and the sun is shining through the open windows onto our sweaty bodies and it's warm and nothing else matters.

$$\triangle$$

Afterward we both glow that postcoital glow as we make brunch together, but Becky also looks sad. She silently makes the omelette while I make the Bloody Marys. She knows it kills me when she looks sad like this.

"I feel like a kid playing hooky from school," I say, somehow trying to cheer her up.

"I do this almost every day," she says.

"Must be great."

"Not really."

I shake the Bloody Marys.

"I didn't get the commercial," she says.

"Good."

"I needed the money."

"It was a stupid commercial," I say. "God punishes those who pervert their talent."

"I don't have my half of the rent this month."

"You should have got the commercial," I say with a smile.

"I know." She's not smiling.

"If it makes you feel any better, I don't have the money to pay my half either," I say.

"What?"

"Try this." I hand her a Bloody Mary. If I can't make her feel better maybe the booze can.

She sips it.

"More Worcestershire?" I ask.

She nods.

I pour it back into the shaker and add more Worcestershire.

"You were kidding about the rent," she says.

"No. I paid off Visa and now I have the choice of paying off American Express or the rent," I say. "For some reason I thought you might be able to cover the rent."

"You've had a lot of strange ideas lately."

"True."

She looks over at the IBM PC, an expensive white elephant I bought after starting work at Big Gun, not expecting to work there any longer than it took me to polish off a new script. For the last few months I've been polishing the first ten pages.

"Think how helpful it's been for writing letters and things," I say, referring also to the letter-quality printer.

I think about how I've grown attached to our consumer goods. I know it's sick. But sometimes I sit and stare at them: the TV, the VCR, the stereo equipment, the computer equipment, and I like how it all *looks*. I know it's sick.

"You should still be writing," she says.

"Yeah, then I'd have gone broke months ago."

"You really should be," she repeats.

"Why?"

"Because."

I shake my head. "I can't imagine why."

"Money?" she says.

I look at her.

"What are we going to do," she asks.

"I don't know."

"Daddy?" She means mine, not hers. She comes from a working-class Minnesota family. We've never actually met, but I have this image of them as stout hearty people, the salt of the earth and the backbone of our country and all that. They're "emotionally" supportive of Becky, but she's supported herself financially ever since she was eighteen and left home for New York City.

Becky hasn't met my family. All she knows is that we're not particularly close and I don't particularly like to talk about it, so I'm surprised she's suggesting I hit my father up for a loan.

"Father's having a midlife crisis," I say. "Took time off from his practice to travel around Europe like Hemingway or something."

"Really?"

"He wants to run with the bulls."

"I hope he doesn't get hurt."

"I hope he's maintaining his life insurance."

I hand her a Bloody Mary.

She sips it. "Good," she says.

I fill her glass all the way and pour myself one.

"What are we going to do," she says.

I haven't exactly cheered her up. "Eat breakfast," I say.

Afterward we do the dishes together. She washes and I use my long arms to dry and put away. We don't talk.

△

On the roof we sun in our lounge chairs. It's blinding bright and we're both wearing sunglasses. Becky's coating herself with Bain de Soleil. She practically squeezes out a whole tubeful. She likes lying in the sun but doesn't like to get too tan.

"Want me to help," I ask.

"I've got it," she says.

She still looks sort of sad, and I want to say something to make her feel better. I pick up her bottle of mineral water. "You can burn ants with this bottle," I say.

"What?"

"If you hold this bottle just right, it acts as a magnifying glass and fries ants or spiders or whatever."

She doesn't acknowledge this. And, because of her sunglasses, I can't tell where she's looking.

I put down the bottle and stare out at the palm trees that are about eye level. "Where would you be now if you could afford to be anywhere doing anything?"

Pause. "L.A.," she says.

"God, now I'm worried about you."

Becky sort of laughs. "But with enough money I'd do any quality movie I wanted and cast myself in any role I wanted."

"Common Hollywood fantasy."

"True."

"Like Miss TV Star's doing in your play," I add.

"Yes."

"And nobody's taking her seriously."

"*She's* taking herself seriously."

"How bad will she be," I ask.

"She might be good."

"No?"

"And if she sucks, she still has buckets of money to cry into."

I laugh.

"You've been working at Big Gun too long," she says. "The whole country isn't as dumb as Big Gun hopes."

"What provoked *that?*"

"It's true."

"Have you seen the box office reports in this week's *Variety?*"

"Well," she says, "I don't know, I just wish I didn't have to worry about quitting the play to take a role in a rock video or something. To play some fantasy slut with linoleum brains."

"You'd quit the play to do something you think is sick and offensive and immoral?"

"For enough money."

"Good point."

Pause.

"Think things would be better if we had more money," I ask.

"Fuck, yes."

"Of course."

"No," she says. "I don't know."

"Wonder how we're going to pay the rent?"

"I'm a little worried about that, too."

"I'm not *worried,*" I say. "I'm just curious."

"I'm worried."

"Don't be."

"I'm not equipped with a button that says, 'press

here to turn off worries, fears, and all other emotions.' "

"You're *not?*" I say. "You should be."

"How do you do it?" she asks.

"What?"

"Turn yourself off?"

"I don't."

"I know you've got emotions in there *somewhere*," she says.

I shrug.

For a long time we just sit there frying in the sun. Becky is feeling no better and this keeps me from feeling much better. We fry silently.

Finally the sun goes behind some clouds.

"Ready to go in," I say.

"I have to move out," she says.

"Huh?"

"I'll start looking for an apartment of my own."

"What are you talking about?"

"Zeke," she says, "you *know* this situation's like . . . caving in."

"Yes, so . . ."

She shakes her head.

"So we're a little late with the rent," I say. "We'll pay it somehow. Maybe I'll get a real job. You know I could make more money as a bartender. And bartending is a good manly profession, and they'll always be in demand, I could—" I realize I'm starting to babble.

If my mother heard her only son who had an almost perfect score on the SATs even *talking* about seeking a job as a bartender . . . it would drive her back to Sylvia Plath.

"The money isn't it," Becky says, "and you know it."

"What is?"

65

"I don't know," she says, "because you won't tell me."

"Won't tell you what?"

"Why you've been acting like this."

"Like what?"

"Something is obviously very wrong," she says, "but if you won't talk about it . . ."

"We're talking now."

"No."

"I saw your lips move."

"You go out and do these weird things to *test* me or whatever and then come back and we fuck, and then you think it's all okay."

Pause. "I *don't* think it's all okay," I say.

"We *fuck*," she says. "It's sad, we just *fuck*. As soon as it became just fucking I should have moved out."

"It's not just fucking."

"It is to *me*."

My throat feels really dry.

"I can't *touch* you anymore," Becky says. "And I keep trying, and you keep . . . turning yourself off."

I have a long swallow of mineral water.

"There's a pattern developing here," she says. "You do these weird things, come home and fuck me, and then we come up here and lie in the sun and pretend nothing's wrong."

I nod. It's a pretty accurate summary.

"It's *warped*," she says.

I nod.

"Are you just going to nod?"

I nod.

Jesus. Am I emotionally retarded or what? Have we de-evolved to the level of dumb beasts?

I look over at her as she gets up. I can see tears

coming out from underneath her sunglasses. My stomach starts hurting.

△

She walks out of the apartment with a duffel bag and a huge purse. I stand alone in my madras shorts. I take a beer from the refrigerator and sit down on the futon and serious depression seizes me.

She's gone.

I tell myself to cope, but my stomach really hurts. I try to think of something happy. I fail. All the things in life I've been told bring happiness: money, security, power, sex, serving a Catholic God who has a sick sense of humor. . . . They must've been kidding.

I have, of course, suspected this was all a joke from the beginning. But recently everything seems particularly pointless.

Maybe I should get mercilessly drunk and go to a tattoo parlor and have NO FAITH etched on my forehead. Or maybe on my ass, so no one will see it. Or maybe on my penis. Maybe I'm just losing my mind.

Rock and roll. There's always rock and roll. I think about putting on a CD. The Cure's "Boys Don't Cry," maybe, but no, the Cure are too nocturnal. Won't work during the day. Velvet Underground? No, I'm stopped dead by a memory of Lou Reed posing like a geek in a Honda scooter commercial. The Plague has even wormed its way into rock and roll.

I walk into the bedroom and rummage through Becky's drawers until I find what I'm looking for: a Baretta handgun that Becky's parents mailed her after reading a story in *Reader's Digest* about the dangerous scum of Venice.

I fondle the hard dark smooth steel. Just like a

gun's supposed to be. It's the same gun James Bond used in his first movies, so I do a James Bond pose in the mirror, then find myself doing DeNiro in *Taxi Driver*.

"You talking to me? You must be talking to me 'cause I'm the only one here."

Suddenly I point the gun at my temple. I've often wondered what this would feel like. It's much easier than I expected. Holding the gun like this strikes me as comical for some reason and I laugh. It's a nervous laugh, and it sort of scares me.

I look at the reflection. Then I point the gun "right between the eyes." This just makes me cross-eyed.

I try opening my mouth and shoving in the barrel. This seems like something a psychiatrist would label latent homosexuality, so I pull the gun back out.

Finally I get smart and check the magazine to make sure the gun isn't loaded. I close my eyes and point the gun at my temple. I pull the trigger—*TICK*.

I feel goose pimples popping up.

Opening my eyes, I eject the empty magazine, then go into the bathroom and look in the cabinet above the toilet where Becky keeps the bullets. I reach onto the dark top shelf and feel what I think is the box of bullets. But as I pull them out I knock over a bottle of pills and as I try to catch the pills I drop the bullets into the toilet.

The toilet is filthy, too.

Standing with the gun in one hand and the pills in the other, I stare at the bullets in the toilet.

Then I hear a key in the door. I put the gun in my back pocket and put down the top of the toilet and sit. It's not comfortable.

"Zeke?"

"In here."

The bathroom door is open. Becky looks in. She's carrying the duffel bag and purse she left with. "Why are you sitting there," she asks.

"It's comfortable."

Pause.

"I just drove around," she says. "I didn't know where to go."

"Stay here."

"Only until I find someplace else."

"Sure."

"I'm not just saying that."

"I know."

Pause.

"I'll find someplace within a week," she says.

I nod.

"I *will*," she says.

"I know."

Pause.

"I'm going to get dressed for an audition now," she says.

I nod.

"For chrissakes, Zeke, why don't you *do* something?" she says. "Watch a movie or something."

"Okay." I remain seated.

She looks at me.

"What are we going to do about our stuff," I ask. "The TV's technically yours."

"I don't give a fuck about our *stuff*," she says and walks away.

I close the door and fish the bullets out of the toilet.

△

69

I rummage through our videos: *American Graffiti, Bonnie and Clyde, The Breakfast Club, Easy Rider, Apocalypse Now, Animal House, Five Easy Pieces, The Hustler, Meet John Doe, It's a Wonderful Life, On the Beach, Saturday Night Fever, Sleeper, The End, Annie Hall, Vanishing Point, On Golden Blonde, The Graduate,* and then find the movie I'm looking for.

I put *One Flew Over the Cuckoo's Nest* into the VCR, open another beer, and start some popcorn. Just as the movie starts Becky comes out of the bedroom and heads toward the door. She's wearing a black leather mini-skirt and one of my white button-downs. She looks sexy as hell.

I put the VCR on pause. "Where are you going," I ask.

"An audition," she says. "I told you."

"Oh, right."

She turns to leave and I'm about to start the movie, then she stops. "What are you watching," she asks.

Pause. *"Cuckoo's Nest,"* I say.

"Cuckoo's Nest?"

As a small irrational protest, I've always refused to watch this tape of hers. I once saw Ken Kesey on the only hip television show and Letterman asked Kesey if he'd ever seen the movie version of *Cuckoo's Nest.* That, Kesey said, would be akin to watching your daughter get gang-raped by the Hell's Angels.

Becky knew all this and was looking at me funny.

"I've always wanted to see it," I confess.

"Why'd you change your mind?"

I shrug.

She looks like she might scream or something but just exits silently.

I hit the remote control and let the movie roll.

△

After the movie finishes, I stare at the screen for a long time.

Big Chief gets his freedom. But first McMurphy has to get his lobotomy and die. An upbeat ending. It makes me feel something and it makes me see something and it makes me want to do something noble and worthwhile, or at least strangle a Big Nurse.

It's a great movie—almost half as good as the novel.

I don't think Kesey's daughter was raped by the Hell's Angels. Unlawfully fondled, perhaps.

△

Absolutely beat, I lay my head down and try to sleep. I'm hovering in that half-conscious not-quite-asleep and not-quite-awake state. More than a few times this is where I've encountered the answers to all my questions, but I usually just fall asleep and forget them.

This time, however, I'm getting out of bed with the answer.

I call my life-insurance company and ask them to change the policy my grandparents started for me so that Becky, rather than my parents, will be the beneficiary. The man says they'll mail me the necessary paperwork.

Quite taken with my cure-all idea, I come back to bed and feel myself falling asleep.

Like a baby with a bottle of Scotch.

ACT

II

I'm shaken awake and my first thought is *major earthquake*. God has finally decided to dump California.

"Zeke, Zeke! It's time to wake up."

This is no earthquake.

"Wake up, Zeke."

There's a stranger in my bedroom. The afternoon sun is coming through the window behind him like overblown backlighting, and I can't make out the face.

"Time to wake up."

I know the voice. "Y.J., what the fuck——" I'm cut off by my own coughing attack.

Y.J. moves out of the sun's backlighting and hands me a beer. One of mine, several hours old. When I sit up and drink, the coughing is squelched. So I light a cigarette and offer Y.J. one.

"I don't smoke anymore," he says.

Y.J. is wearing basically the same thing he was wearing when I last saw him a couple years ago: a white T-shirt, black blazer, holey Levi's, and Lennon specs with dark lenses.

I have another long swallow of the warm, stale beer. I offer Y.J. the can.

"I brought it in for you," he says.

I keep the beer and finish what's left. I'm groggy as hell. "What day is it," I ask.

"Friday."

I feel like I fell asleep only moments ago. "I've got to get some sleep," I say.

Y.J. shakes his head.

I lie down and close my eyes and try to go back to sleep. But these thoughts are coming to me—something about suicide, yes, I'm going to kill myself.

As I ponder this a calmness comes over me. Peace in our time, at last.

But Y.J. turns on the radio-alarm and Billy Idol is yelling. *"And there's nothing sure in this world, and there's nothing pure in this world . . . start again . . ."* Y.J. cranks it.

I sit up and turn down the music. Then I focus my eyes and notice there's a white dog sitting on my pants.

"Come on, Blackie, remove yourself from Zeke's wardrobe," Y.J. says.

The dog moves.

"Blackie?" I say.

Y.J. nods.

"What's a dog doing in here," I ask. "And what the hell are *you* doing in here? How'd you get in?"

"Door was unlocked," he says, "I knew you were here."

"The door was *not* unlocked," I say, "and how'd you know I was here?"

"It was unlocked."

"So how'd you know I was here?"

"You're here, aren't you?"

This is how conversations always go with Y.J., so I lie back down.

"Come on, Zeke," he says, "we've got *multitudo* to do."

"*Multitudo?*"

"A *multitude,*" he says. "You haven't forgotten flunking Latin together, have you?"

"I've tried."

I look at him and he raises one eyebrow and I laugh. Ogvassed has always made me laugh.

"We've got *multitudo*, huh?"

"Yes indeed."

The white dog woofs at me.

△

Y.J. wants to mingle with the masses, so we wander into the boardwalk throng, blasters, dancers, comics, musicians, roller skaters, and the exhibitionists and the voyeurs and everybody else just hanging out.

Venice is the only place in L.A. where a confused person on drugs might think he's in Greenwich Village, if he doesn't notice the beach. Y. J. seems to like it here.

The diapered guy who carries the ten-foot cross is out today screaming for the crowds. "*If any man worship the beast and his image he shall be tormented with fire and brimstone.*"

"He's insane," I point out.

"How do you know?" Y.J. asks.

"Look at him," I say. "Listen to him."

"*Watch yourself and pray always that you will be worthy to escape all these things that shall come to pass. . . .*"

"Makes perfect sense to me," Y.J. says.

77

Actually, it almost does make sense and that worries me.

"This way," Y.J. says, walking toward the Sidewalk Cafe.

"What have you been doing with yourself," I ask. "I keep getting these vague postcards from strange places."

"I've been traveling."

"I figured that much."

Pause.

"What brings you to L.A.," I ask.

"You."

"Me?"

"I knew I could count on you for a few free meals," he says.

△

We're eating Heuvos Rancheros and I'm working on my third margarita while Y.J. is drinking his second red wine. I haven't put this suicide thing into perspective yet and I think it might help to verbalize it. The tequila seems to agree. "I'm going to commit suicide," I say and take a big gulp of my drink.

Y.J. nods.

I light a cigarette.

"Camus said the only important question in life is whether or not to kill yourself," Y.J. says.

"He died from smoking nonfiltered cigarettes."

"Is that how you plan to do it?"

"No," I say. "Too slow."

"So what's your plan?" Y.J. says. "Jump off a bridge? Slit your wrists? Hang yourself? Shoot yourself? O.D.?"

A touristy couple nearby is eavesdropping, so I lean in close. "I don't want to make a public announcement."

Y.J. leans in even closer. "How are you going to do it?"

"I don't know yet."

Pause.

"But you think you can really do it," he asks.

I nod.

"Why?"

"I don't know," I say. "For a while I've been thinking, Why not? What reason do I have *not* to? But since I had no reason *to* do it, it was your basic standoff."

"But now you've found the reason?"

"Yes."

"This should be amusing. What?"

"You mentioned Camus."

"Yeah?"

"Well," I say, "remember when we decided the moral of *The Plague* was you're either for or against the Plague."

"Yeah. We were seventeen and stoned as rats."

"Yeah, well, it's been coming back to haunt me lately. I'm starting to realize that somehow I've become *for it*."

"You're *for* the Plague."

"I don't *want* to be for it, but I just am. I've been part of the things, the Plague."

"Oh, yes," Y.J. says, "the *things*."

I nod.

"So you're going to kill yourself?" Y.J. says.

"That's the plan."

"Wouldn't it be easier to just switch sides," Y.J.

asks. "Be against it. Carry a sign around that says, 'I'm against the Plague.' "

"I don't think I can redeem myself by just carrying around a sign."

"Re*deem* yourself?" Y.J. says. "*Oh,* we're talking about redemption."

"That's part of the idea."

"By offing yourself?"

"Well . . ."

Y.J. starts grinning.

"I'm not *joking,*" I say. "Think about it. What's the ultimate act of love?"

Y.J. takes a sip of his wine, then says, "Sacrifice."

"And what's the ultimate sacrifice?"

"I get the idea."

I nod and sit back.

"Hell," Y.J. says, throwing up his hands in mock surrender, "I'm convinced. Kill yourself."

"I intend to."

As the tourists get up to leave, they look at the two of us like we're criminally insane.

"How do you think Rebecca will react?" Y.J. asks.

That makes me lean back in. "Becky," I say. "And how do you do know about Becky?"

Y.J. performs one of his mock-enigmatic gestures. "The actress you've been living in sin with," he says.

"Where'd you hear that?"

Y.J. smiles. "I suppose she'll get the insurance money?" he says.

"Yes," I admit, and Y.J. nods.

Pause.

"I'm just waiting for some paperwork," I say.

"When do you expect to fill it out?"

"Monday."

"And when do you plan to do it?"

"I don't know. That night, I guess."

"The same night. Don't you think that's going to look a little strange?"

"Stranger things happen all the time. As long as they can't *prove* it's suicide."

"Monday, huh?" Y.J. says.

"I guess so."

"Good," Y.J. says. "Good. That gives me time to work on you."

I shove my food aside and light a cigarette while I wonder why Y.J. seems so pleased.

"Work on me?" I say.

"Three days until Monday," Y.J. says. "Possibilities . . ."

Pause.

"You think you can talk me out of it," I say. "Don't you?"

"That's not what I said," Y.J. says. "Maybe by trying to talk you out of it I'm actually going to talk you *into* it."

Y.J. smiles his mischievous smile and finishes his wine. I don't know what to say, so I signal the waiter for our check.

"I don't have any money, you know," Y.J. says.

"Of course."

I turn to watch the variety of people passing by on the boardwalk. I wonder how many of them think about killing themselves.

The check comes and I put my American Express on top.

"This is going to be . . . feral," Y.J. says.

81

I've forgotten what feral means.

$$\triangle$$

We're walking again among the masses on the boardwalk.

"What inspired all this," Y.J. asks.

"What?" I say. "You mean the suicide?"

Y.J. nods.

"I don't know," I say. "Everything."

"You seem pretty cool about it."

"Cool?"

"You seem pretty much in control," Y.J. says. "I'd think a guy talking about killing himself would be *out* of control. But then again you were always out*standing* at acting like you were in control. Never fooled me, but everybody else."

"Don't try to analyze it."

"Why not? I've got nothing else to do."

"This isn't a logical idea," I say.

"But you're acting like it's logical."

"Am I?"

"Yeah."

"Well," I say. "I know it's not logical. But that doesn't stop me from having these feelings."

Y.J. gets this look and starts singing like Barry Manilow or someone like that, *"Feelings, whoa, whoa, feelings . . ."*

A few people turn to look at us.

"Sorry," he says, still laughing, "I couldn't help myself."

I nod and try not to smile.

"Okay," Y.J. says, trying to seem semiserious, "you've been thinking about this a lot."

I nod.

"And you think killing yourself for love is a sound idea."

"Seems like a good gesture."

"I see."

"A *noble* gesture."

"Uh-huh."

"I don't have any reason *not* to."

"Uh-huh."

"And," I say, "it is a far, far better thing I do—"

"—I get the idea," Y.J. says. "We're dealing with a spiritual crisis."

"A spiritual crisis?"

"A lot of that going around," Y.J. says. "It's an epidemic."

"I haven't read about it in the papers."

"Nobody wants to start a major panic."

"Of course."

Y.J.'s head suddenly spins, and I look where he's looking: a stunningly beautiful tan girl in a red and black one-piece floats past on roller skates.

We look back at each other and I'm glad I caught him.

△

We walk along the ocean, and for a long time neither of us says anything. There are a lot of seagulls making seagull sounds.

"I can't even see a seagull anymore without thinking of that goddamn book," I finally say.

"*Jonathan Livingston Seagull.*"

"Yes."

We go a few more minutes without saying anything.

"Can you get me a ticket to this Sunday night's preview of *Waiting for Godot,*" Y.J. asks as we turn back toward my apartment.

"What?"

"Becky's play," Y.J. says. "I'd like to see it with you."

"Okay."

I haven't mentioned this to him, and I refuse to ask him how he knows.

△

As we come down the apartment hall I see Becky standing outside our door. She looks confused.

"There's a white wolf in the apartment," she says.

"A coyote," Y.J. says.

This does not seem to relieve Becky.

"It's a pet," I explain. "A pet dog."

"Whose," Becky asks.

"Mine," Y.J. says.

"Becky," I announce, "this is Y.J. Ogvassed."

"And that's Blackie inside."

△

Y.J. takes Blackie out for a walk while I stay inside with Becky.

"Who the hell is *he?*" she says soon as Y.J. pulls the door closed behind him.

I don't answer because I've just realized something: Y.J. has assigned me a suicide date.

"Who *is* he?" Becky repeats.

I let him do it. In fact, I *encouraged* the bastard. "I

don't know what to tell you," I say, locking the door. The sun is about to set outside the window and Becky seems like a goddamn goddess and even if there's no connection it's a nice combination and I suddenly have this avid urge for sex.

I walk over and start kissing her.

"What's this daytime sex stuff," she asks as she pulls back.

"Get it while you can," I say.

We start kissing and fondling, but Becky's nose begins twitching and though I initially think this is some atavistic female thing she spoils the thought by pushing me away. "Look!" she says. "The wolf shit on the floor."

I look and yes, Blackie did indeed shit on the floor.

I scoop it up on an old *Hollywood Reporter* and dump it in the toilet. Then I start to clean the spot on the floor with Windex.

"Windex is no good on hardwood," Becky informs me. She gives me a soapy sponge to use. She stands over me to supervise.

"Zeke? Who is this guy with the wolf?"

"It's not a wolf."

"Who the fuck is he?"

"An old friend from boarding school."

I finish the floor and throw the sponge in the sink.

"Don't put that in the sink!" she says. "Throw it out."

"I read somewhere that animal shit is actually much cleaner than human shit."

"Throw it out."

I throw it out and wash my hands.

"Let's go back to where we were," I suggest, "before he comes back."

85

I try to help her undress, but she pulls away and gets out the Cuisinart to make one of her health milkshakes.

"Is he *staying* here," she asks.

"I guess so."

"What do you mean?"

"Yes," I say, "I think so."

"You don't know?"

"We didn't discuss it specifically."

"Who is this guy?"

"I told you," I say, "I was good friends with him in boarding school. The one after Our Lady of the Lake."

"Why haven't I ever heard of him before?"

"He sort of drops in and out of my life," I say. "It's been a couple years since I saw him."

"And where might that have been?"

"Visiting my mother at the nut house."

"Oh," she says.

Pause.

"Well, what's he doing here now," she asks.

"He's . . . visiting, I guess."

"Where's he live?"

"I don't know."

"It doesn't sound like you know him very well."

"He's one of those people you're really close to, even if you go a long time without actually seeing."

"What's he do?"

"For a living?"

"Yes."

"I don't know."

Becky just looks at me as she loads the Cuisinart with nuts and fruits.

"Even in school I never really knew much about

him," I explain. "He claimed his parents were hippies who made him live in a commune but the commune got busted and he was packed off to an orphanage. At the orphanage they discovered he had this phenomenal I.Q. and sent him to ol' Saint Luke on some scholarship. He never really told anybody much about himself. I don't even know what the Y.J. stands for. And he made Ogvassed up—he thought it was funny at the time."

"He seems a little peculiar."

"He is."

"So he's staying here?"

"Looks that way."

Pause.

"You've already found a new roommate," she says.

"No," I say. "He just showed up."

"I guess I'm really not in a position to complain." She turns on the Cuisinart.

"Do you want me to turn him away?" I ask.

"No."

"I will if you want me to."

"No, it's your apartment. Do what you want. I'll be gone soon."

"I'll ask him to leave, if you want."

"No."

Pause.

"Why does he have a wolf," Becky asks.

"It's a dog," I say. "Part coyote but mostly mutt. Blackie."

"Is Blackie staying here, too?"

"Apparently."

"Is Blackie going to shit on the floor a lot?"

"I'll ask him to use the toilet."

"Y.J. or Blackie?"

"Both."

"Thank you."

"You're welcome."

Becky turns off the Cuisinart, pours her concoction and drinks it down.

I try again to help her undress. She declines.

"I'm going to the bathroom," she says.

"Can I come with you?"

"No." She smiles, which means, Yes, if I wait a couple minutes.

I use some tequila to refresh my mild buzz.

When I hear the shower come on I go into the bathroom and undress.

"I feel so scummy every time I get back from Hollywood," Becky says. "The air's so filthy."

I open the shower curtain, clear plastic with fake blood splatters and *Psycho* logo, and step into the tub facing her.

She looks at me and smiles. "You're in awfully good spirits today."

I smile.

"Do you have any idea why you have these manic mood swings," she asks.

"I deny that."

She laughs.

I take the soap from her and turn her around so I can lather her backside.

"I shouldn't have let you in here," she says. "There must be something wrong with me."

Drawing in the white soap lather with my finger, I outline an eye.

"What's that," I ask.

"I don't know."

I repeat the shape with my finger.

"A circle," she says, "with a hole in the middle."

"An eye," I say.

"An eye?"

"Yes."

I draw a heart next.

"What's that," I ask.

"A heart?"

"You're getting the idea."

I draw a four-legged animal next.

"What's that," I ask.

"Do it again."

I do it again.

"Again."

I do it again, but my hand wanders—

"Hold on," she starts to say.

—but both my hands have a hold now and she's turning to face me and my hands are moving with her and we're kissing and I'm saying something about a ewe and she's chewing on my ears and neck and we go down in the tub under the warm falling water.

I try to forget about feeling anything but this.

△

We join Y.J. and Blackie in the ocean. The sun has set, and the twilight waves are small and close together. We stand around waiting for the right wave to body-surf in on. It's cold and we're all shivering a little and I'm sobering up.

"You're an actress," Y.J. says to Becky.

She nods.

"*Waiting for Godot*, right?"

She nods.

"How's it coming," Y.J. asks.

"Okay," she says and dives under a wave and swims off.

"She doesn't like talking about her work much," I tell Y.J.

"Why?"

"I'm not exactly sure," I say. "Happens if you live in this town."

Becky suddenly grabs me underwater and surfaces into my arms.

I think how much I'm going to miss this, but then I realize I wasn't really enjoying it until I made the decision to leave it and this hits me as sort of sad and sort of funny and absolutely appropriate. The word *ironic* comes to mind and, because I hate that word, I laugh.

"What's so amusing," Y.J. asks.

"Everything."

"That's a good sign."

Becky looks at us strangely.

"No body-surfing on heaven or hell," Y.J. says.

I shrug to Becky.

I wonder if Y.J.'s right about a spiritual-crisis epidemic. If he's right, things are worse than I suspect. If he's wrong, I'm worse than I suspect. Have a nice day, Zeke.

A good set of waves finally shapes up, and we all ride into the shore on the same one.

△

After we all shower, separately, Y.J. cooks a dinner of wild rice mixed with a medley of vegetables stir-fried in red wine.

We sit down to eat with a couple more bottles of red wine.

Blackie sits a few feet away and drools politely.

"This is excellent, Y.J.," I say. "I'm glad you've learned something these last couple years."

"Yes," he says, "I've learned to eat."

"What else have you been doing," I ask. "Besides learning to eat."

Y.J. stuffs his face with a forkful.

"Your postcards don't give much away," I say.

Y.J. keeps eating.

"This is *really* good," Becky says.

Blackie whimpers softly.

When Becky looks at the dog, it cocks its head— so cute I think it knows what it's doing.

"Shouldn't we feed the wolf?" Becky says.

"Don't let her fool you," Y.J. says, "I fed her already."

"She looks hungry," Becky says.

"She likes what we're eating," Y.J. says. "Blackie used to be human."

I keep eating. Becky stops, trying to decide if Y.J.'s funny or just weird.

"Of course," Y.J. adds, "that was several lives back."

"Of course," I say.

Becky looks at me and I shrug.

"She's an incredibly enlightened soul," Y.J. says.

I fill up Becky's wine glass.

"You might think it's strange," Y.J. says, "that an enlightened soul should have to regress from human form to animal form."

Now Becky realizes Y.J. *is* being funny, but she's still not sure if he's kidding.

Neither am I. "I could see how someone might think that's strange," I say.

91

"The thing is," Y.J. explains, "it's not necessarily a regression. Souls choose whatever form will help them learn whatever they're after, and in some cases the human form might not be as serviceable as an animal form."

"So," I say, "I guess this explains the postcard from India."

"No," Y.J. says, "Started dallying with reincarnation here in the midst of Western pop culture."

"Anyplace in particular?"

"Several places."

Pause.

"I guess I started exploring the possibilities at the seminary," Y.J. says.

"The seminary?" I say. "You were studying to be a priest?"

"Yes."

"Excuse me if I sound shocked."

"You're excused."

"You were studying to be a priest?" I repeat.

"Yes."

"Why didn't you tell me?"

"I didn't want to talk about it," he says. "I'd just gotten the boot."

"They kicked you out? Of a seminary?"

"Just like all the other schools," he says. "They asked me to leave."

"Why?"

"Pretty much the same reason as all the other schools."

I turn to Becky. "Y.J. was kicked out of Saint Luke for slipping magic mushrooms into the soup one day. Got the whole school stoned." I turn back. "You didn't do that at the seminary, did you?"

"No," he says. "Maybe I should've."

I look my plate, particularly at the mushrooms. "You didn't," I say, "did you?"

"What?"

"What kind of mushrooms are these?"

Becky tentatively tastes hers.

"Just mushrooms," Y.J. says.

"Where'd you get them," I ask.

"Zeke," he says, "they're just mushrooms."

"Plain old-fashioned mushrooms?"

"Plain old-fashioned mushrooms."

The taste *is* a little strange. I look at Becky and this time she shrugs at me. "So," I say to Y.J., "what did you do after you left the seminary?"

"Traveled."

"Where?"

"Places. I met Blackie on the road. I immediately knew this dog was an enlightened soul when I asked her name and she said Blackie."

"The dog told you its name was Blackie?" Becky says and turns to the animal. "Is this true?"

The dog cocks its head.

"She didn't *say* Blackie," Y.J. explains. "She put the name in my head."

"Oh."

"Telepathy."

"Right."

"The dog can levitate and speak in tongues."

Pause.

"Just kidding," Y.J. says. "She can't really levitate and speak in tongues. She *told* me she could, but I've never actually seen her do it. I suspect she was just reeling me in."

Pause.

"What was the question?" Y.J. says.

"Where you traveled?"

"Here," Y.J. says, smiling. "Here we are."

"Yes," I say.

Pause.

"I think I might have been the Pope in a previous life," Y.J. says.

Pause.

Y.J. laughs.

"Y.J.," I say, "I have to admit I never could tell when you were bullshitting."

"What's to bullshit about," he asks.

"Yes," Becky says, "what's to bullshit about."

"This guy is not Pope material," I say, pointing at Y.J. "He looks silly in hats."

"Not anymore I'm not," Y.J. says. "I've progressed *beyond* the Pope."

I cough, then guzzle some wine. I hope God isn't listening to this.

"Don't you believe in reincarnation," Becky asks me.

I suddenly realize she's into this. "Are you two *both* getting weird on me?"

Becky smiles.

"Becky," I say, "do *you* believe in reincarnation?"

"Sort of."

"Sort of?"

"I've always believed I have a soul."

"Okay," I say, "but that doesn't mean you believe in reincarnation."

"I believe my soul goes *somewhere* after I die."

"Okay," I say, "does that mean you might come back as the Pope?"

"It's possible."

"You never told me you had these weird ideas before."

"I find it a little hard to believe you don't believe in reincarnation," Becky says, smiling.

Y.J. is also smiling.

"Hold on here," I say. "I didn't say I didn't believe in reincarnation."

"*Do* you believe in reincarnation?"

"No."

"You don't."

"No," I say, "but I don't *dis*believe in it, either. I don't know. And neither do you."

"What do *you* think happens when you die," Becky asks me.

"I don't know."

"What do you *think?*"

"I suppose I'll be buried. And people will come to my funeral and talk about what a wonderful human being I was and then get drunk and party. I'll miss a good party."

"I see you've given this some heavy thought," she says.

"How do you know someone else doesn't know what happens?" Y.J. says.

"It can't be known."

"How do you know it can't be known?" Y.J. says. "If it can't be known, you can't know if it's known."

"Fuck off."

"I *know* God exists."

"Congratulations."

Y.J. laughs. "Aren't you going to tell me *that* can't be known?"

"Okay," I say, "it can't be known."

"Of course it can't be known."

"Interesting argument."

"*Nothing* like that can be known."

"Uh-huh."

"But we *act* as if certain things are true and through our faith make them true."

I look at my food. "I'm catching a bit of a buzz," I say, "and I'm a little suspicious of these mushrooms."

"For example," Y.J. continues, "if I talk to Blackie as though she understands me, and I *feel* better because she understands me, then she *has* understood me. I know she's understood me because I feel better."

"Uh-huh."

"*Adeste Fideles.*"

I don't know exactly what Y.J. means by this, but I remember the phrase from a Christmas carol. "I think we should feed the dog," I say.

△

We're still drinking when we lie on the fold-out futon to watch my tape of this season's first "Saturday Night Live" with Madonna as the guest host. It's exactly the sort of show the original would've viciously satirized.

We enjoy talking about how bad and unhip it is, except for the Yuppie Hell bit, and then I put on a tape of the very first SNL. Michael O'Donoghue is playing an English teacher to John Belushi's dim student:

"Good evening," O'Donoghue says.

"Guuuuuud eve-ning," Belushi says.

"Good evening," O'Donoghue says. "Let us begin. Repeat after me . . ."

Belushi dutifully repeats a few mildly amusing lines. Then O'Donoghue has a heart attack and falls over dead. So Belushi has a heart attack and falls over dead.

"Live from New York! It's Saturday Night." Then a commercial comes on and none of us are sure if it's a parody or not.

△

I don't know if it's the booze, the excessive smoking, the lack of sleep, the staring at the TV, the conversation, the presence of Y.J., or possibly even the mushrooms, but by the time "Saturday Night Live" finishes I'm beyond buzzed and moving toward pleasantly deranged.

"Let's do something," Y.J. suggests.

"I don't feel like doing much right now," I say.

"I can't talk you out of this if you don't at least give me a sporting chance."

"Talk him out of what," Becky asks.

Pause.

"Fatal sensitivity, sadness, and confusion," Y.J. answers.

"Fatal sensitivity, sadness, and confusion?" Becky repeats, then gleefully smiles. "That's what life's all about!" Becky likes her wine buzz.

Y.J. fills everyone's glasses.

"If the phone rang now and somebody asked you to do something, would you do it," Y.J. asks me.

"What?"

"If the phone rings in, oh, about thirty seconds, will you take that as a *sign* and ride it out?"

"What are you talking about?"

"The phone is going to ring, and you'll be asked to do something. Do it."

Becky and I look at each other.

"Deal?" Y.J. says.

97

"If that phone rings in thirty seconds . . ." Becky laughs.

She doesn't know Y.J.'s tricks like I do.

"Zeke?" Y.J. says.

I should know better, but I nod affirmatively.

"You'll do it?" Y.J. says.

I nod.

We watch the phone, sip our wine.

I can't remember how many times Y.J. has pulled off quasi-mystic shit like this, but often enough to make me think there's a distinct possibility the phone will ring on cue. And I'm confident there's an earthly explanation that he won't tell, but he never explains himself so I'm never sure.

A minute passes before anyone says anything.

"You're losing your touch, Y.J.," I say.

"It's only been a minute," he says.

"You said thirty seconds," I point out.

"Did I say thirty seconds?"

"Thirty little ones," Becky says.

"I meant thirty *minutes*," Y.J. answers.

This, I remember, is the key to his mystic success: stay vague. I often wonder if Y.J., given his many gifts, will someday be elected President of the United States and Leader of the Free World.

"The deal was for thirty seconds," I say.

"*Deal?*" Y.J. says. "Did we make a deal?"

Before I can answer the phone rings. Becky laughs and Y.J. smiles.

I pick up the receiver. "Hello?"

"Zeke," Wendy yells over the phone, "can you hear me?"

"Yes."

"What?" There's loud disharmonious music in the background.

"Yes," I yell, "I can hear you."

"I'm at Tibet," she yells. Meaning the club, not the country. "Susie's filling in for a band tonight. In about thirty minutes. You should come. Hurry."

"Well," I say. "I—"

"See you soon," Wendy yells and hangs up.

I put the receiver down.

"A deal's a deal," Y.J. says.

"A friend of mine's doing a poetry reading or something at Tibet," I say to Becky.

Becky looks at Y.J. and he smiles.

"You boys go ahead," she says.

I look at Y.J., expecting him to insist that Becky join us. He doesn't.

"You sure?" I say to her.

"Yes," she says.

"Come on."

"No," she says, "I have some things I should do."

"Like *what?*"

"I should probably study my script."

This doesn't sound like Becky.

"We better hurry," Y.J. says, "Susie goes on in thirty minutes."

I don't ask him how he knows. But I notice Becky is looking at him differently.

△

Traffic is heavy. It's past midnight and everyone knows where their children are—right in the next lane.

"Think of it as a quest," Y.J. says.

"Think of *what* as a quest?"

"A good reason not to kill yourself."

"I'll settle for a good reason to go to Tibet. Susie's poetry is torturously bad. Though, of course, that's the way she wants it."

"Remember hide-and-go-seek?"

"Yes?"

"One of the first places you looked was where they *wouldn't* be, thereby narrowing down potential hiding places."

"Working on your analogies, huh?"

"Highest form of reasoning, according to ol' Aristotle."

"A sodomite."

"True."

Pause.

"Why the Greek stuff," I ask rhetorically.

"We're on a quest, are we not?"

"Of course."

△

Susie is already onstage when we arrive in this warehouse with chairs. Smells like cheap wine and stale beer. A few of the hard-core, including Wendy, are sitting down in front. We stand with the majority on the periphery leaning against walls.

Everyone except me is wearing black. I feel like asking a few what they're mourning but I'm afraid I know.

Susie is rolling:

> *"fuck you and your threats*
> *fuck your cock-shaped pastel lipsticks*
> *I prefer the color of black and blood"*

Cheers from the front rows.

"fuck you and your promises
fuck your cock-shaped bottles of perfume
I prefer the smell of formaldehyde"

The end.

Big raucous humorous cheers.

"This next one," Susie says, when her friends and fans shut up, "is for all of us who come to this place."

There's actually a polite semisilence.

"there's this place
you come to
'cause you heard
from Dick and Jane
and your friends
the usual penisbrains
that it's cool
way way cool
now and hip
hap-happening
and this means
a place you might find something
so you come
and you're here
and you see
it's just the same
old story
yes, you fucked up again."

More cheers.

"but you try
next weekend
a new *place*
'cause they all say

> *this is it*
> *and you're willing to believe, hey—*
> *might be true*
> *so you come*
> *it isn't*
> *and you don't care*
> *'cause by now*
> *you just want a chocolate eclair*
> *what the fuck*
> *next weekend*
> *call some friends*
> *buy lots of booze*
> *drink heavy*
> *then at least you'll be coming drunk"*

Wild cheers. Partly facetious and partly not. A few frenzied fans offer Susie drinks, pills, and joints.

Susie gratefully accepts everything, her due.

During this chummy break, she sees me and waves. When Y.J. and I wave back, Wendy turns around and spots us and gestures for us to come forward. Despite Y.J.'s urgings, I decline.

Susie slaps the microphone a couple times. This makes an annoying noise and draws everyone's attention. "I'd like my partner in crime from Big Gun, Zeke, to come up here and read the next one with me," Susie booms out.

Cheers.

Practically nobody here knows who I am, but no matter, they're clapping anyway and Y.J.'s pushing me and Wendy's shouting at me and Susie's luring me up with a bottle of Scotch, but I am not drunk enough to buy into it.

Susie and Wendy and Y.J. all know I don't believe

in making a public spectacle of myself. Cool habit prevents such a thing. But I suddenly realize cool habit is ridiculously unnecessary for someone who plans to be embalmed in the near future.

I try to shut out this image and the smell of formaldehyde and join Susie on stage and take a swallow of the Scotch. The crowd goes nuts.

I wonder what I'm doing here? I take another, longer, swallow. The crowd fucking *loves* it.

I imagine how performers must feel.

"This is something Zeke and I sort of wrote together one day when we were supposed to be working," Susie tells the audience as she unwads a piece of paper from a pocket in her leather jacket. "It's called, 'Isn't it fucked?' "

I have done many things with Susie, but never once composed verse. But I decide to play along and act poetic.

Susie starts reading:

"isn't it fucked
that we don't know
and we have to wait so goddamn long
and isn't it fucked to live all alone
in the kind of world where we don't belong"

She stops and points at my lines. I read:

"you wonder if it can be much worse
that big black day in the hearse"

Susie picks it up:

"isn't it fucked
alone at night

103

feeling so bad and so goddamn old
and isn't it fucked to be crying
with nothing and no one to hold"

I start to remember having a hand in this as Susie
points at my lines:

"I wish every fuck was excusing
everything we've been losing"

Then we start reading together:

"maybe if we drink and pray and lie and die
it might come true
ha, ha, ha
there's only one thing we can do"

We smile.

"too bad we don't know what it is"

Some laughs. Then loudly:

"you know the more we laugh about it
it makes it worse to live without it
so let's laugh about it
oh, isn't it fucked"

Susie and I both cough when we finish.

A glorious eruption of approval. Van Halen doesn't
get this much drunken adulation. Susie is delirious and
jumping all over me. I keep cool.

Part of me wonders what everyone's so goddamn
excited about. Another part likes it.

△

"Bad poetry for a bad world," I say later to Y.J.

We're in a dark corner with Susie and Wendy and other nefarious types. Somebody is saying something about Somerset Maugham, something about love and art being the only worthwhile things in life.

Somebody else is talking about the prophecies of Nostradamus, and evidently the world should be coming to an end around 1996. The only person who argues about the end of the world is a guy with SAVE ME tattooed on his hand, and he swears the Bible sets the Second Coming around 1998. Everyone seems to accept that the end is near.

"So," I say to Wendy and Susie, "what are you going to do about it?"

They all look at one another and smile or laugh or seem confused.

"We're *doing* it," Susie says.

Wendy holds up her beer. "To doing it until the end," she says.

Everyone holds up his beer and drinks.

"I think I should get back to Becky," I say to Y.J.

"Noooooo," Susie and Wendy yell in unison.

"Yeah," Y.J. says, "you probably should."

Nobody argues with Y.J.

"You coming," I ask him.

"Noooooo," Susie and Wendy yell in unison.

"I'll be there in a couple hours," he says. "The gals will give me a ride, right."

"Right," the gals yell in unison.

The way Wendy and Susie are looking at Y.J., I think he may get a ride but not to my place and not in a couple hours.

△

Becky is lying on the bed reading her script. She's wearing one of my white button-downs. I sometimes think she moved in with me just so she could wear my shirts.

"You boys have a good time," she asks.

"Yes."

"Good," she says. "Where's Y.J.?"

"I left him with Wendy and Susie."

"Sounds fair."

Here's a perfect chance to communicate. I'm still feeling hyped up and there are things I should say, but instead I start undressing. I can feel my heart beat for some reason.

"You still haven't gotten even with me," I say.

"For what?"

"For my binge," I say, as I walk over and sit on the mattress in my boxers. "You haven't exploded yet."

Becky takes off her shirt, *my* shirt, and lays it on the floor. "I don't explode," she says.

"True," I say, "you usually punish me with the silent treatment."

"I don't *punish* you."

"Yes," I say, "you do." I slip in under the covers.

"What do you consider punishment," she asks.

"Whatever *you* need to do to feel better."

"No," she says, "I only do it so *you'll* feel forgiven afterward."

"Then you admit it."

"Yes." She smiles.

She takes off her white cotton panties, which she doesn't always do for bed, and kisses me. While we're kissing and touching I ask her in a teasing whisper if she'd like to tie me up. She shakes her head with a smile, but I ask her again and she pulls back to look at me.

106

She goes to the closet and returns with a belt and two of my ties. One's a school tie and I almost object but that would kill the mood, for sure.

Neither of us says anything as she pulls the covers back and ties my left wrist to one corner of the brass bed frame she inherited from her grandmother. She ties my right wrist to the other corner. Though she's not Boy Scout snappy with the knots, I'm patient.

With both hands she grabs the waist band of my boxers. "Up," she says. I raise myself and she strips the boxers off. She ties my legs together with the belt and secures them to the middle of the end of the frame.

She steps back and smiles very strangely at me.

I feel sort of like I did when I first had sex.

I wonder if this is sick or only strange. Or maybe even normal. Are people all over the world seeking for-giveness through recreational bondage?

Her fingers tickle the palm of my left hand and then start spider-walking up my arm, over my shoulder, across my head, and down the other arm to my right palm.

I've got mountainous goose bumps.

Her fingers do the same walk up my left leg all the way to my navel and then walk back down the other leg.

She crawls onto the bed and sits on my stomach and draws designs on my chest. I'm watching and she reaches out and runs her fingers lightly over my eyelids to close them.

I feel her lips start kissing very lightly on my shoulder, nibbling and blowing warm air as she comes down my chest, and *biting* at my stomach. I have a passing panic that this teeth trend might continue, but the biting becomes licking and the gentle nibbling and blowing recommence.

I give in completely, thinking I deserve much worse.

△.

When I wake up, it's still pretty dark.

For a moment I wonder if maybe an entire day has gone by, but I see Becky and the ties and belt and decide I only slept a couple hours. I'm not quite yet hungover, but I still feel like shit. Trying to stand, I'm struck down by that massive lethargy that makes it impossible to do anything more demanding than rest, but won't let you sleep.

Whatever high I was on is gone. Naturally. This is the worst I've felt since Y.J. appeared.

While it doesn't look like he's doing a very straight job of dissuading me from suicide, I know I shouldn't think about that right now because right now I'm very vulnerable to bad thoughts.

I literally crawl into the kitchen. I don't *need* to crawl, but I feel like crawling so I crawl. Y.J. and Blackie are crashed out together on the futon. I wonder what happened, but I'm not prepared to wake him and find out.

Instead I tank down several glasses of bottled water.

"Replenish those precious bodily fluids," Y.J. says. I remember the line from one of our favorite movies, *Dr. Strangelove.* This thought slightly cheers me up.

"Bottled," I say, "no fluoride."

"Good."

"Why are you on your knees," Y.J. asks.

I stand up slowly and lean against the Sparkletts water cooler, which promptly falls over and floods the room. I watch for several seconds before righting the cooler and plastic jug. I stare at all the water.

"If it was a little colder out," Y.J. says, "we could go ice skating."

I get a sponge and a roll of paper towels and start cleaning up.

"Need any help?" Y.J. asks.

"No, thanks."

"Good."

I start a flood-control clean-up system. This is the most satisfying work I've done in years.

"Sorry," I say. "I didn't want to wake you."

"I wanted you to," he says. "We've got a lot to do."

"Where are Wendy and Susie?" I ask.

"God only knows."

"They drop you off here?"

"Yes."

"And?"

"And here I am."

"So what happened?"

"We made plans."

"Plans?"

"Yeah." Y.J. stands up and gets dressed. "But that's for the future and it might not even happen. For now, you've only got another seventy hours and we've got *multitudo* to do."

"Now," I say, "I don't particularly feel like doing anything."

"Yes you do."

I shake my head negatively.

But after astounding myself with a truly regal floor-cleaning job, I feel a little better and agree.

△

We're sitting in my convertible shortly before sunrise, top down. I haven't started the car yet because I don't know where we're going.

"I love this light," I tell Y.J.

"Why?"

"I don't know. Makes me glad I'm not asleep."

Y.J. nods. We watch the blue glow spread across the eastern horizon.

"You can do anything now," Y.J. says.

"Like what?"

"Anything," Y.J. says. "Anything you ever wanted to do you can do now. You *have* to do now."

"Anything?"

"Possibilities . . ."

"Well," I say, "I don't know where to start."

"You have to have a lifetime in the next seventy hours."

"That's going to be tough."

"It's going to be *fun.*"

"I can't think of anything particularly fun I want to do."

"What *can* you think of?"

"Nothing."

"What do you mean?"

"If I could think of a lot of things I wanted to do, we wouldn't be in this jam, now would we?"

Y.J. nods.

I play with the steering wheel and for no good reason have a flash memory of a Disneyland ride.

"What seems important to you," Y.J. asks.

"Nothing."

"Right," Y.J. says. "Nothing *is* important."

I nod.

"Except for what's important," Y.J. adds.

I roll my eyes. "Where are we going," I ask.

"You're really in love with her."

I nod.

"These are troublesome times for lovers, huh?"

"No shit."

"How do you think she's going to feel," Y.J. asks. "You being dead and all."

"She'll feel better when she gets the money."

"You really believe that?"

"I don't know."

"If the insurance company figures out what happened, all she'll get is a 'sorry, your boyfriend blew it' letter."

"I thought of that, as I already told you."

"So you know how to make it look like an act of God or a simple fuck-up?"

"Not yet I don't," I say. "But I will."

Pause.

"You *really* think the money will make any difference to her?"

"I don't know." I fiddle with the radio knobs. "We were about to break up."

"Untimely death will certainly solve *that* problem," Y.J. says. "Why were you going to break up?"

"I don't know," I say. "I guess we just reached that proverbial place where you either take the next jump or break up."

"And you'd rather break up?"

"No," I say, "but that's what was happening. And I couldn't seem to do anything about it."

"Why not?"

"I don't know."

111

Pause.

"You know," Y.J. says, "I saw this coming seven years ago when you told me "A Perfect Day for Banana Fish" was the greatest story ever written."

"It *is*."

"I saw it coming."

It's getting noticeably lighter out.

"Let's go," I say.

"Right," Y.J. says. "Let's go."

"Where?"

"Doesn't matter. Let's just go."

I put on some phony Ray Bans I keep in the glove box and start the car and Y.J. puts on his Lennon specs and turns on the radio. Together we drive into the smog-blue light.

△

We're driving past Marina Del Ray as the sun starts to come up.

Y.J. turns down the radio. "You want one of those boats," he asks, pointing at the thousands of bobbing boats. "We could borrow one, preferably a sailboat."

"Steal one, you mean."

"Right," he says, *"you* can do anything. You'll be dead soon. Deader than a two-dollar bill."

"Deader than a two-dollar bill?"

"Indeed. So why not steal a sailboat?"

"I do not want to steal a sailboat."

"How about murder?"

"Murder?"

"Aren't there some people you'd like to kill off before you go? Some movie people maybe?"

"Yes," I admit, "but I'm not about to start murdering people, *especially* not now."

"What about just beating the holy shit out of a few?"

I turn the radio back up.

"I was just curious," Y.J. yells over the music.

We're soon flying down the Pacific Coast Highway and the Go-Go's are on the radio. *"How much more can we take before we go crazy here. . . ."* and when the song is over a traffic report comes on and I switch it off.

I feel a euphoria starting to swell. I'm confident it will pass.

△

Rush hour in L.A. runs from six A.M. till three A.M.

We drive back into the city at seven A.M. I'm coming up on a light that's about to turn green, and to my right I can sort of see a yellow Porsche speeding up to catch the yellow and the driver talking into his cellular phone and I know I should slow down but I keep my foot steady on the gas and enter the intersection just as the light turns green and the Porsche runs a red and rips my right front fender and careens off spinning into a bus stop with plastic ad posters that shatter.

Somehow during this I hit my own brakes and pull the car over. I sit and hold my legs. Adrenalin is pumping up from my feet in huge electrical surges. A good buzz.

I look at Y.J. and he looks at me. For less than an instant I catch in his eyes something other than the usual enigmatic sparkle, but he looks over at the Porsche and the bus stop and when he looks back at me he's himself.

I wonder how long this adrenalin rush will hold out.

The police arrive and the Porsche driver, while

straightening his tie—which he probably thinks is "new wave," tells the cop he's a busy studio president. The cop writes him a ticket.

"I just realized who he is," I say to Y.J.

"He's *for* the Plague?"

I nod.

The cop lets me go. The studio president has to wait for a tow truck. As we drive away, I look at him talking on the cellular in his totaled Porsche.

△

My whole-wheat bread pops up perfectly toasted tan. I butter it. The adrenalin has dropped me down and I'm very hungry. Ships coffee shops are brightly lit and every table has its own old-fashioned electric toaster.

My legs still feel a little strange.

"I'm worried about your soul," Y.J. says.

I heap orange marmalade on my toast.

"It's bound to be looking for a new home soon, and I doubt you've properly prepped it for the search."

"I refuse to discuss my soul at Ships."

"Where would you like to discuss it," he asks. "Church?"

"No."

"I think we should discuss it in church."

"I'm not going to church."

"What's a church?"

"What?"

"*This* could be a church. A church is just a building where people agree they're going to momentarily honor something good about themselves they call God before they go out and act like assholes again. It could be done here just as well."

114

"And" I say, "people could eat breakfast at the same time."

"Right, it would be very efficient."

"Maybe we ought to call the manager over here," I say. "I think this is high-concept."

"No, we'd better test it first," Y.J. says, grabbing the toaster off the shelf by our table. "We'll be pioneers." He plunks the toaster down on the table between us. "Think of this as . . . something holy."

I nod and chew my toast at the same time.

"And think of this fork as your body and this knife as your soul," he says, slipping the knife blade between the fork prongs.

The waitress delivers my eggs and sausage and Y.J.'s orange juice. I use my own knife and fork to eat.

Y.J. frowns. "Do you know what's in that sausage," he asks.

"No."

"Imagine what pigs eat."

"What do pigs eat?"

"*Slop.*"

"So you're saying I'm eating slop."

"Second-hand slop."

I keep eating.

"You're poisoning your fork," he says.

"My fork."

"Your body."

"Right."

I quit eating.

"But right now," Y.J. says, "I guess we're more worried about your soul."

"The knife."

"Right," he says. "And when you die they bury the fork."

115

"Or cremate it."

"Whichever. But your *soul*, the knife, what happens to that?"

"They put it in the dishwasher?"

"Okay," he says. "Let's say they put it in the dishwasher. And something goes wrong and the knife gets chewed up by the blades. So they throw out the knife. And it's compacted into garbage. And then it's thrown into an incinerator. Then it's gone."

"Life's a bitch. Then you die."

"But it isn't gone. This knife is made up of atoms." He starts waving the knife around, which seems to disturb some nearby patrons. "And the atoms are held together by *energy*. And energy cannot be destroyed, only transformed. So the energy of this knife is going to become heat and smoke and rejoin the air."

"Your basic smog problem."

"Yes, and your soul's going to do the same thing."

"Become a smog problem."

"Rejoin."

"I think you ought to quit waving that knife around."

He does. But then he starts semirhythmically tapping it against the toaster.

"Rejoin what," I ask.

"Whatever you want to call it."

"You mean the Big Guy."

"Or that Great Party in the Sky. Or the Great Big World of Unified Atoms. Or the Ultimate Green Eggs and Ham. Whatever you want to call it."

"I don't want to call it the Ultimate Green Eggs and Ham."

"Make your own moniker."

"How about Hell?" I ask. "How do I know next stop for my soul isn't Hell?"

"Some would say that's the chance you take with suicide. You might find yourself in a worse situation than you're already in."

"What could be worse?"

"Oh, *plenty.* I think you can imagine."

"Okay," I say. "But what if I'm doing it for a good reason?"

"Becky."

"Right."

"What if you're fucking up?"

"Then I'm fucking up," I say. "Surely the Big Guy can forgive a little fuck-up."

"Why should He? If He knows you know you're fucking up."

"Well," I say. "There's also the chance that when I'm dead I'll just be dead."

"Maybe," he says. "Care to bet on it?"

The waitress comes by. "Need anything else?" she says.

"He needs a reason to live," Y.J. says, gesturing to me.

"If it's not on the menu," she says, "we don't have it."

I smile and she winks at me as she clears our plates away.

"Ever read Elizabeth Kübler-Ross," Y.J. asks me.

"Is she that life-after-death quack?"

"The very one," Y.J. says. "She interviewed all these people who had been declared clinically dead, heart attacks and drownings and such, but somehow, doctors or good luck, they came back alive. And they had very

similar visions as they were dying—they felt themselves
leaving their bodies and traveling through a tunnel toward
an extraordinarily bright white light."

As Y.J. pauses, I take out a cigarette and play with
it.

"The light is supposed to be this indescribable
warm comforting force," he continues. "The light asks,
nonverbally, of course, these questions. Like, what have
you learned, what kind of wisdom have you gained, have
you learned to love? That sort of thing. And, quite
frankly, Zeke, I'm afraid you're going to stand there and
say you don't particularly know. It'll be embarrassing for
you."

I light the cigarette.

"I think you need some guidance," he says. "So
today we roadtrip up to Big Sur. I know where we can
rendezvous with a UFO and get the help you so desperately
need."

"Are you aware that you're losing your mind?"

Y.J. grins at me like a madman. "I'll make you a
deal," he says. "If I *can't* talk you out of suicide by
midnight this Sunday, I'll take the trip with you."

"What trip?"

"I'll kill myself, too."

"That's a truly idiotic idea."

"But it makes perfect sense."

I look at him doubtfully.

"If you *do* this," he says, "if you feel it's right, then
maybe it *is* right, or at least maybe it's *leading* to something right. And if that's true, then it's right for me to be
a part of it, because I'm here and therefore that must be
why I'm here."

"I'm really worried about you."

"I'm worried about *you*."

"Is this male-bonding, or is this male-bonding?"

Y.J. laughs. *"Acta Sanctorum,"* he says.

"What?"

"Just kidding."

He's apparently amused by my ignorance of this dead language.

The waitress brings the check and I pay.

We walk out to the car, and I stop to stare at the crunched right fender of my Ken and Barbie car. Wires from the smashed headlights dangle purposelessly. It makes me feel like everything's so goddamn fragile.

△

Becky is playing tag with Blackie when Y.J. and I get back. "You didn't leave me a note," she says.

Blackie runs over and slobbers on Y.J.

"Sorry," I say. "I thought we'd be back before you got up."

"You probably would have," she says, "except the wolf came into the bedroom and woke me."

"We're roadtripping today," Y.J. says to Blackie, who woofs her enthusiasm.

"Do you have rehearsal," I ask Becky.

"No," she says, "director gave us the day off. Today I rest."

"Today you play," I say.

"Today I rest."

"We've got a rendezvous tonight," I say. "Out of town."

"We do?"

"I'm going to introduce you to some interesting friends of mine," Y.J. says. "Orgonians."

119

"You want to drive to *Oregon?*"

"No," I say, "Big Sur. His friends are extraterrestrials."

Becky looks at Y.J., who nods on cue.

"They're from the Orgon galaxy," he says.

Becky looks at me.

"Dress casual," I say.

△

Becky is standing in her oversized men's thrift-store overcoat, staring at the right front fender.

I proceed to load the car with a picnic lunch, a couple blankets, a cooler with a six pack, one bottle of white wine, and three bottles of red. Y.J. is having a chat with Blackie.

Becky can't stop staring at the car. Then she looks at me, at Y.J. and at the dog, looks again at the car, then looks back at me.

"Something went crazy in the cosmos," I say. "Some molecules just *snapped* or something, and that fender scrunched itself up."

△

It's a great day for a drive. The offshore wind on the Pacific Coast Highway is cool but not cold, the sky is clearer than usual, and because it's technically fall the beaches we pass seem strangely deserted.

Radio reception is already bad, but when KROQ plays Duran Duran Becky turns it off.

We live without music for a while. And without talking. I can sometimes hear the waves over the sound of the engine—it's a good feeling and I think the same thing I think every time I feel like this: I should do it more often. But I remember this might be the last time, and it feels even better.

Blackie is sitting up on the back seat so she can see everything. She's drooling.

△

As we approach Oxnard we tune in one of these retro stations that play nothing but sixties and seventies "classic rock." Crosby, Stills, Nash and Young sing about needing a code to live by, then the Beatles sing all they need is love.

What's too true or silly to be said can be sung.

I remember reading this on a wall at a party in a thrashed Hollywood house known as "Disgraceland." Wendy and Susie told me about the party. They never showed up. But a girl named Pleasant saw me reading the wall and explained that most of the graffiti had been scrawled for the benefit of a reporter who said he was with *Rolling Stone* and researching his article, "A Lost Generation—Or a Nothing Generation?"

Pleasant, a Disgraceland resident, even showed me a copy of the article, which ended up being published in an airline magazine. She laughed as she pointed out all the lies.

This reporter later decided to become a screenwriter.

The Beatles fade out, Joni Mitchell starts singing about circle games, and I pop in The Replacements and fast forward to "Here Comes a Regular." This is always good for an instant depression.

"Am I the only one who feels ashamed . . ."

△

Mark Lindquist

Once we reach Route 1 we pull over and arrange ourselves on a blanket on the sand and eat the bread and cheese and drink the wine out of glasses Becky brought along.

The salty froth of the breaking waves flies on the wind all the way to our faces. I can taste it. The wine and afternoon sun keep us warm.

I try to think of words for this mood—euphoric, idyllic, halcyon, joyous, bliss, beatific—

—"melting mood," Y.J. says.

"What?"

"Melting mood," he says. "I stole the phrase from William James during my rabidly religious phase. James thought that during these moods we're more open to noble and holy thoughts."

I'm a little spooked by his interjection.

"Have you seen *Meatballs*," Y.J. asks.

I nod. This is more comfortable territory.

"Bill Murray has this great line," Y.J. says. " 'It just doesn't matter anymore.' "

"The basketball game scene."

"Says it all."

"*Awful* movie," Becky says.

"Yeah," Y.J. says, "but Murray would probably be a hell of a good guy to get shitfaced with."

△

My mind wanders as I drive, and I keep envisioning this crazed mailman alone on a bicycle built for two.

I decide to concentrate on the countryside.

I traveled through several countries during my misguided postcollegiate searching phase, but I've never seen anything more spectacular than Big Sur. My eyes

122

stray from the twisting hillside road and out over the cliffs down to the sunset reflecting in the faraway green water.

To drive off the edge would be very easy. And very tempting if it weren't for my three passengers.

△

We're listening to another retro radio station and a live version of "Like a Rolling Stone" comes on. The concert crowd is roaring when the chorus comes and we roar along with them, *"How does it feel. . . ."*

And the crowd's roar rises into a cathartic frenzy and we've drunk just enough to scream along insanely as though the song is *our* story.

Facetiously, of course.

"They might've been fucked up back then," I say, "but the music was good."

"Must've been a wild time," Becky says.

"Don't fret, kids," Y.J. says. "Our time will come."

"Our time for what?" I say.

Y.J. shrugs.

"Something has to happen," Becky says.

"Like what?" I say.

Becky shakes her head, and Y.J. shrugs again.

"Maybe the ET's will tell us," I say.

"Oh yeah," Becky says. *"That's* what we're doing up here. Maybe they'll even loan us some money to pay the rent."

"Maybe they'll *eat* us," I say.

"Maybe they'll take us back to their planet," Becky says, "as *slaves."*

"Sex slaves."

"You two think I'm joking," Y.J. says.

123

Becky and I look at each other and nod.

"I am joking," Y.J. says, "but the Orgonians aren't."

"Okay," I say, "what the hell is that supposed to mean?"

"They have a different sense of humor than we do."

"The Orgonians?" Becky says.

"Right."

"From the Orgon galaxy."

"Right."

"You just said you were joking about Orgonians," I say.

"Yes, but that doesn't mean they won't be here tonight."

"Y.J.," Becky says, "could you please pass me the bottle of white wine?"

I'm not concentrating on the road, and the car wrenches around a particularly tight turn with a squeal and severe side-sway. For a moment, Becky looks scared.

"Wait until Monday," Y.J. says to me.

"What," Becky asks.

"What," Y.J. asks back.

"What did you say about Monday?"

"I thought you said you wanted the white wine," Y.J. says as he hands her the bottle.

△

The midnight air is cool. The sky is clear and the moon is almost full.

The beam of my one headlight shines out over the thin guardrails into nothing then swings back onto the fluid road and then back out into nothing.

I feel relaxed for the first time in a long time.

A melting mood, maybe.

△

Y.J. tells me to pull over at one of the half-circle shoulders the highway commission built so people can get out of their cars and admire the view while they eat their Big Macs.

When I turn off the engine we can hear the ocean waves coming in hundreds of feet below us.

Becky and I look at Y.J. Y.J. and Blackie are looking around. Blackie jumps out of the car and runs around, sniffing the ground.

"This is it," Y.J. says.

Becky and I look at each other.

"Is there any wine left?" I ask.

"Just red," Becky says. "Or do you suppose the Orgonians prefer white?"

"They don't drink," Y.J. says.

"We're not going to have much in common then," I say, "are we?"

"You'll be surprised."

"I'm sure I will."

I reach into the glove compartment under the religious pamphlets and parking tickets for my flask of Scotch.

"Let's go," Y.J. says.

"I thought this was it," I say.

"It is," he says, "but we have to walk the rest of the way."

"Walk?" I say. "Walk where?"

Y.J. points to the edge of the bluff. I get out of the car and look down. It's steep, and in the few places where

125

there aren't rocks there are thorny shrubs. Though I can't see any snakes, I know they're waiting patiently.

"Wouldn't it be easier for the Orgonians to fly up here?" I say.

"Doesn't work that way," Y.J. says.

"Why not?"

"Ask them when they get here," Y.J. says. "Bring the blankets."

Y.J. slips a bottle of red wine in his jacket, and Becky carries another, and he leads us over the moonlit edge.

The trail isn't as steep as it looked and Y.J. seems to know where we're going, but I know how well he can fake these things.

Though I doubt I could die by tripping and falling, a crippling accident is not out of the question and that, I think, would be worse. So I watch my step. And watch for snakes.

It occurs to me I haven't decided how I'm going to kill myself. I could just jump off a cliff. The coroner's report would list drunkenness as the probable cause and the insurance company would have to pay.

But what if I just *maim* myself? Break a leg? Or break my neck and become a quadriplegic? Fuck. Then I'll be trying to kill myself in the hospital, but without legs or arms I probably won't be able to, so I'll have to ask someone *else* to do it and then it becomes a big court case and Hollywood makes it into a moronic TV movie.

No, this has to be a clean sure death.

I've heard drowning is a good way to go. Somebody at a party told me he'd been swimming in the ocean drunk at night, and an undertow had held him down until he inhaled water. He claimed that once he accepted he wasn't going to make it to the surface, that he was dying, it was ultimate bliss. Then he blacked out. When he woke up on the beach, his buddy and their two girls were standing over him. He was still on earth and he was disappointed. But, the disappointment passed when he remembered he was going to get laid that night.

He didn't say anything about bright lights or voices, though. I suppose he might have made the whole thing up. Or heard it somewhere and said it was first-hand experience so it would make better cocktail conversation.

This is not a solid enough source to inspire me to try drowning.

I wonder if I could drink enough to kill myself. John Bonham of Led Zeppelin did. So did Bon Scott of AC/DC. So did Keith Moon of The Who. So did a friend of mine from school, drunk driving. But all those guys were far more experienced and accomplished partyers than myself. I'd probably just wake up with a hellish hangover.

Cancer is slow and unreliable and painful.

But maybe I can smoke enough in the next couple days to completely clog my lungs and suffocate.

How are other people going to feel about this? It will ruin my father's European escape. Maybe. And maybe it will shock my mother back into sanity. Maybe not.

And people like Wendy and Susie and Bob Cutler will get over it okay, Wendy and Susie will probably *benefit* from the vicarious experience.

There's just Becky and Y.J. to worry about.

Actually, there's just Becky.

Will she *understand?*

"What are you thinking?" Becky says, right on cue as usual.

"Was I thinking?"

"What are you thinking?"

"I'm just trying not to fall off this goddamn cliff."

"You were thinking about something."

She can almost always tell and I almost always deny it.

"Well," I say, "are you pretty excited about meeting the Orgonians?"

She glances at Y.J. and back at me and rolls her eyes. We both laugh. Then we look around and back at each other.

"It's a gorgeous night out," she says.

"Yes."

Will she understand?

And if she does, how will she feel?

Fuck. I'm going to have a leave a goddamn suicide note absolving her. How the hell do you *write* something like this? When you got a C in freshman comp.?

Δ

Y.J.'s trail leads us to a sheer rock and a twenty-foot drop.

"We've got a problem here," I point out.

"No we don't," Y.J. says as he jumps.

He lands, does a couple somersaults, and rolls up onto his feet with the bottle of wine. "Geronimo," he says.

"I think you're supposed to say 'Geronimo' *while* you're jumping," I call down to him.

"Show me," Y.J. says.

While Becky and I hesitate, Blackie jumps. She lands on her feet and runs to Y.J., then barks a couple times.

"You're supposed to say 'Geronimo' *while* you're jumping," Y.J. tells her.

128

"What the hell does 'Geronimo' mean," Becky asks me.

"It's the name of an Indian."

"Yes," she says, "but why do people say it when they jump."

"I don't know," I tell her. "Y.J., do you know why people say 'Geronimo' when they jump?"

"Because other people do."

"Thanks."

Becky and I stand at the edge gazing out.

"This really is beautiful," Becky says.

I nod.

"Ready to jump?" she says.

"Ladies first."

Becky takes my hand and pulls. We jump together and the sand is much softer than I expected.

△

It feels like we've entered another world. Behind us is a cliff, on either side are enormous boulders we can't see around, and in front of us the white path of moonlight across the ocean.

"Is anyone else bothered by the fact that we seem to be trapped here," I ask.

"We're not trapped," Y.J. says.

"We can't go back the way we came."

"There are other ways back."

"I hate to think how much walking this will involve."

"You've been in L.A. too long."

"No argument there."

I sit down and take off my shoes. Becky does the same.

"What now?" she says.

"We wait," Y.J. says.

"Is this going to be anything like *Close Encounters of the Third Kind*," I ask.

"No."

"What *will* it be like?"

"Wait and see."

"My mother always used to say that to me—Wait and see."

"Before or after she lost it?"

"How long do we have to wait?"

"No way of knowing," Y.J. says, "but this gives you time to prepare your questions. And your requests."

Y.J. lays out one of the blankets and we sit Indian style, except for Blackie, who sprawls. We pass my flask around.

"You've talked to these, uh, Orgonians before, huh?" Becky says.

"Yes," Y.J. says. "Of course."

"And they answered your questions," she asks.

"Some of them."

"What did you ask?"

"I can't tell," Y.J. says. "You have to come up with your own."

"I was just curious," Becky says.

"Ask them anything you want."

Pause.

"I want to know what other kind of life there is out there," Becky says.

I turn to Y.J. "Did you ask them that question?"

"Yes."

"Then why can't you tell us," I say, "and save the Orgonians the trouble."

"I think everyone needs to hear it for themselves."

"What are *you* going to ask?" Becky says to me.

"You mean *if* I really had the opportunity, what would I ask."

"Yes," Becky says.

"Don't be so sure you *won't,*" Y.J. says.

I do not expect to be chatting with Orgonians tonight. I feel like a kid at camp by the small fire in the night listening to ghost stories and being sure they aren't true but enjoying being scared that they *might* be.

"I'd ask what the fuck it all means," I say.

"That's kind of vague," Y.J. says. "If your question is confused, you're likely to get an equally confused answer."

"Why am I on this hellish planet?"

"That's still kind of vague."

"I want to know what my *mission* is," I say. "I want to feel like a saint who *knows* what's important and what he's supposed to do."

"I'm not sure you're ready for that."

"Thanks."

"Maybe you should ask some questions about time and build up to questions about your future. Based on what you learn about time."

"I feel like I'm back in school—"

"Well—"

"—with an acid-casualty professor."

Y.J. shrugs and grins.

"We could ask if there was a Jesus Christ," Becky says. "And what his background was. That's *history*. They could answer that, right?"

"I would think so," Y.J. says.

Pause.

"Are these Orgonians *connected* to us in any way," Becky asks.

"This is starting to sound like a rerun of 'To Tell the Truth,' " I say.

"Ask," Y.J. tells her.

"We could ask about the Big Bang," I say.

Becky and Y.J. both give me dirty looks.

"Seriously," I say. "We could ask about how the universe started. *That* right there would answer a lot of other questions."

"I suppose if the Big Bang theory is true, then we *must* be connected to the Orgonians," Becky says.

"Not quite first cousins," I say, "but connected nonetheless."

Becky laughs and asks, "How long have they been coming to this planet?"

"Ask the ones who know," Y.J. says.

"I can think of lots of questions to ask," Becky says.

I notice that she's starting to ask these facetious questions as if she means them, and I wonder if she actually does in some way.

"Do you two have any requests," Y.J. asks.

" 'Stairway to Heaven,' " I say.

"I loved that song once upon a time," Y.J. says.

"So did I," Becky says.

"Me too," I admit.

We look at each other sheepishly and laugh.

We go on about matters cosmic and how the questions and requests might best be phrased, but it starts to get chilly and we run out of alcohol so we lie down and put the second blanket over us and snuggle up.

I'm very curious about what's going to happen to

me when I die. Will the light at the end of the tunnel really pull a pop quiz on me?

I know I'll miss nights like this.

△

I wake up when it's still dark and Becky and Y.J. are still asleep.

I've just had a dream.

I was in a U-Haul pick-up or something with Molly Ringwald. She was driving. But there was something very wrong: she was driving down a twisty mountain road in reverse while looking forward.

"We're going too fast," I said.

I don't know why I didn't tell Molly she ought to either look in the direction she was driving or turn the truck around.

"We're going too fast," was all I could say.

I don't know if she heard me. The Smiths' "Please please please let me get what I want" was playing very loudly on the radio and Molly was into it.

Humming the tune, she pulled a huge tube of pink lipstick out of a shopping bag and painted her puckered lips while she looked in the rearview mirror and the truck squealed and groaned and tilted around these tight corners above sheer cliffs.

I kept cool and was proud of it.

Even when the Teen Queen took both hands off the wheel to rustle her red hair while steering with her knees, I kept cool.

"We're going to die," I said calmly.

She just pouted and smiled at me with those pretty in pink silicon lips like, "What, *me,* Molly Ringwald, die?

133

No way!" And kept humming and speeding backward down the hill without looking.

For some reason I felt this enormous affection for her as we went into a hundred-and-eighty-degree turn and went flying off the edge.

Molly didn't notice this.

So I told her. "We're flying off a cliff," I said.

"No way!"

Then we crashed and the truck exploded and I was suddenly standing at a party by a swimming pool in some backyard trying to explain why I got to live and Molly had to die.

"I don't know," I kept saying, "it just happened this way. Maybe Molly should've worn her seatbelt."

These strangers made me feel wretchedly guilty, and then I wake up.

This dream calls for analysis, but I'd rather just go back to sleep. I need sleep more than introspection. I concentrate on the rhythm of the waves and Becky's breathing.

△

The sun is out but we're still in the shade. I wake up and Becky is calmly studying me.

"Morning," I mumble.

"Good morning."

I look around. Everything looks much different in the day. The tide is way out.

"God," I say, "I had some strange dreams last night."

"So did I," Becky says.

My throat hurts and I manage a hearty morning cough.

134

Becky reaches into her overcoat and pulls out a bottle of mineral water.

"You're a genius," I say.

"I'm glad you're starting to notice."

After drinking some of the water, I hand it back and see that Y.J. isn't on his piece of the blanket. "Where's the lunatic," I ask.

"Swimming with Blackie."

I look out over the water but can't spot him. "Where'd he go?"

"Around that point."

It's cold as hell out there, I'm sure, and I cuddle up closer to Becky.

"He's *very* peculiar," she says.

"Very true."

"We should get someone to introduce him to Shirley Maclaine."

"I'd be afraid of what he might do to her."

Becky laughs.

"What did you dream about," I ask.

"I don't exactly remember," she says. "But it was strange. What about you?"

I remember the first dream pretty clearly, and there's some vague memory of a second dream featuring Elizabeth McGovern.

"Nothing," I say, "just the usual subconscious babble."

Becky nods.

"I guess the Orgonians were a no show," I say.

We both laugh.

I decide to try to go back to sleep.

△

135

Y.J., dried and dressed and looking refreshed, joins Becky and I while we're lying half-awake under the blanket.

"Well?" he says.

"Well what?" I say.

"Do you want to talk about it?"

"About *what?*"

"The Orgonians."

"What's there to talk about?"

"You don't *have* to tell me."

"Have to tell you what?"

"What you asked," Y.J. says. "What they said."

I look at Becky, who sticks her head under the blanket.

"Y.J.," I say, "they didn't come. Remember?"

"Oh," he says. "I thought maybe they came after I went to sleep."

"Afraid not."

"Good," Y.J. says. "You shouldn't expect Orgonians to answer your questions for you. Figure them out yourselves."

His glare is facetiously righteous—at least I *think* it's facetious—and then he turns and walks away.

I bury my head under the blanket with Becky. We titter like kids. By the time we pull our heads back out from under the blanket there's no sign of him.

"I think we're alone," I say.

She nods.

I smile at her. She's knows there's a morning missile in range and she knows the smile is a warning siren.

"I hope you don't think this changes things," she says.

"What things?"

"You can be the most sensitive sweetest person sometimes, but I know when we go home you'll . . . turn yourself off."

I shake my head in what I hope is a reassuring manner.

"I *have* to move out," she says. "You know that."

"I don't know."

"Yes, you do," she says. "I have to."

I shrug.

"You understand," she says, "don't you?"

I shrug again.

"I want you to understand," she says.

"I do."

"You do?"

"I do."

"It was starting to hurt too much."

Pause.

"The way it was," she adds.

"I know."

Pause.

"Can I kiss you anyway?" I ask.

She closes her eyes and shakes her head.

△

She's riding on top of me with her shirt and shetland and socks still on.

When her head goes back and her eyes close, I take the opportunity to look around. Ocean waves, big rocks, seagulls, sun coming through haze. This is what morning should look like.

I don't know why I've never done it outdoors before.

It makes me wonder how many other good things I've been missing.

△

Afterward we run nude into the small morning waves. It's cold as sin but it feels good anyway. I can't recall the last time I felt this awake. Or this sober.

Soon enough we run back to the blankets to dry off, warm up, and get dressed.

"I've got to be at the theatre by three," Becky says.

"No problem."

"From this back to the theatre," she says.

"Yeah?"

"Yeah."

"You ever think of throwing cold water out into an audience," I ask. "They're there to feel, so . . ."

"I'm sure it's been done," she says.

"Or maybe have the cast go into the audience with baseball bats and beat the shit out of them?"

Becky laughs. "Feeling aggressive this morning, are we?"

"I don't know why I said that."

"I worry about you sometimes," she says, smiling.

I feel like telling her about the suicide, but I don't know how. We finish dressing and fold up the blankets.

"I suppose we should go find our trail blazer," I say.

"He *was* joking about the Orgonians," Becky says, "wasn't he?"

"Who the hell knows."

"Does *he?*"

"I don't know."

138

"Interesting."

"Yes."

"I hope they don't put him away."

△

We find Y.J. crouched by a tidepool. It's filled with very small fish, small crabs, starfish, and mussels. He's watching something in there intently.

"Look," he says. "Watch these three crabs."

Two medium-sized rock crabs, with their pincher claws thrust out, maneuver around each other for an advantage. A smaller crab, backed into a neutral corner, has lost one of his pincher claws and a couple legs.

"Watch them do what?" I ask.

"Watch."

After much jockeying around, each fighter clamps onto the other's claws. The third crab tries to make a run for it, but he's crippled and not very fast and the other two quickly force it back into the corner.

"What's going on?" Becky says.

"They're fighting over the guy with the one claw," Y.J. says. "He's supper for the winner."

"The one-clawed guy already seems to be short a couple legs," I say.

"Why are we watching this?" Becky says.

"*This,*" I say, "is drama."

"Come on," Becky says, "I've got to get back."

"We've got plenty of time," I say.

We keep watching. Neither of the larger crabs seems to be gaining much of an advantage.

"What round are we in," I ask.

"Last, I think," Y.J. says.

"Have you identified the contestants?"

"The smaller one who still has both claws is Rocky," Y.J. says. "It's the larger one who started it."

"Rambo," I say, and Y.J. laughs.

Rocky and Rambo are in a crustacean standoff while the one-clawed crab cowers in his corner.

"I guess that makes the one who's going to be eaten Sylvester Stallone?" I say.

"This is sick," Becky says.

"You can stop it," Y.J. says. "Anyone of us could reach in with a stick or whatever."

None of us make a move to stop it.

Rocky and Rambo go into the claw-clinch again and again Sylvester tries to make a run for it. But this time Rambo reaches out and grabs one of Sylvester's legs and tears it off. Sylvester counters with his one claw. But suddenly Rocky's pincher gets Sylvester's in the joint and tears it off.

Sylvester crawls back into his corner, totally at the mercy of the other two.

Rocky and Rambo face off. But instead of going after each other they edge sideways toward Sylvester. With their pointy eyes still fixed on each other, they attack separate sides of Sylvester.

Sylvester loses two more legs. He slumps into the sand.

I wonder if he realizes he's good as dead. I wonder how he feels about it.

"This is really sick," Becky says.

"This is drama," I say.

"I don't want to watch."

"You don't have to."

She continues watching.

The jockeying goes on and soon Rambo wins control of the territory. He uses one of his pinchers to flip Sylvester over onto his back. Rambo's claws begin jabbing and ripping into Sylvester's soft-shelled belly. Sylvester's legs twitch.

Rocky has clearly thrown in the towel.

Rambo stuffs his little slit of a mouth.

"All he needs is some melted butter," I say.

△

After a ridiculously long hike we get to the car and start driving back toward L.A. Nobody says much at first. Feels good to be back on the road, but there's something vaguely disturbing about the direction we've chosen.

Though I don't know what the hell else other direction we could choose.

△

In a small town, we stop at a pizza place and order a large tomato-and-olive and a pitcher of beer.

The place is filled with families and video games. The kids who aren't playing video games or running around are staring at MTV on a large screen. Some of the parents catch themselves also staring at it, jerking away at a commercial or a veejay's inanities. But the kids continue to goon away obliviously.

I watch as a gorgeous module dances like a drunk giraffe and drools over an average-looking rock and roller who's wearing make-up not quite thick enough to conceal his pock marks. I stare as this segues easily into a

141

commercial starring the same module. The selling of the Plague.

"I think about Susie's *Star Trek* creature."

"What are you watching?" Y.J. asks.

"What?"

"Why are you watching?" Becky says.

I snap back to life. Our beer has arrived. Y.J., in fact, is pouring me a glass.

"Nothing," I say.

"You can watch that trash at home," Becky says.

"I don't *want* to watch it at home."

"Then why watch it here?" she says.

"Good question," I say.

Is there a special hell reserved for suicides, where you're strapped down like in *A Clockwork Orange* and made to watch rock videos? With Satan as your friendly veejay?

I drink half my beer in one swallow, then light a cigarette.

I feel more like a Scotch. I want to be numbed.

"Television is interesting," Y.J. says. "If you have time to watch the decline of western civ."

△

The traffic starts fighting back at Santa Barbara. We're stuck behind an ancient exhaust-spewing station wagon with a surfboard rack and a bumper sticker that says GOD IS COMING AND BOY IS HE PISSED OFF!

Becky is a little worried about time. I promise I'll get her to the theatre before opening curtain and start speeding and passing cars on the 101.

I turn on the radio and Led Zeppelin's "Communication Breakdown" is playing and I start tapping the steering wheel and this feeling I used to get when I was first starting to drive comes back to me: the urge to push my foot down hard and watch the speedometer needle climb and the scenery blur until I smash through to the other side. Whatever that means.

I don't mention this to my passengers.

I wish I could remember if this feeling started before or after I saw *Vanishing Point*.

△

By three-thirty we're in downtown L.A. But for the derelicts standing outside the liquor stores, it might as well be a fresh neutron-bomb test site.

We race toward the theatre through the empty urban streets and sitting at a corner is a police car I don't see until I'm shooting past at about sixty and my eyes catch the cops' eyes for a flashing moment.

"Now we're fucked," I say, slowing down.

"You can say it's an emergency," Becky suggests.

Somehow I don't think the cops will buy it. But I never find out because apparently these cops have bigger worries than kids speeding in an old American convertible. They stay at their corner and I drive on.

△

We arrive at three-thirty-nine. "A full twenty-one minutes before curtain," I say.

But Becky is already out of the car running into the theatre. The theatre is Jake's Bar. Bohemian bastion by night, bastardized theatre by Sundays.

I park the car, and try to figure the odds it will be

stolen or merely vandalized, but then I realize we're going to have to leave Blackie out here and I feel it'll be safe.

Y.J. ties Blackie to the steering wheel and whispers something in her ear.

"I think they filmed *Repo Man* around here," I tell Y.J. as we walk toward the entrance.

"Good movie."

"Yes," I say. "Very strange."

"Not nearly as strange as this."

"I think that was the point."

"The movie *had* a point?"

"I think so," I say. "And that alone makes it strange."

We're comped into the theatre/bar where a couple dozen people are milling around on the dirty cement floor and drinking.

"This is a bar," Y.J. notes.

"Yes," I say. "Except on Sundays when it's art."

"Looks like a bar to me."

"The stage is in the other room," I say, "where the bands usually play."

"I like it."

We get a couple beers in plastic cups at the bar. Dark, hot, humid, smoky, it smells like concentrated humanity. While Y.J. walks around to check it out, I start eavesdropping on a couple next to me. They're arguing about some movie. The girl says it's too "male oriented."

Y.J. comes back. "I just read a real interesting bathroom wall," he says.

"No shit?"

"Seriously," he says. "You still a bathroom graffiti aficionado?"

"Not like I used to be," I say, "but sometimes."

144

"Then you ought to go in there and catch up on your reading."

But then the lights flash and it's showtime.

△

Becky told me very little about this production. But I suspect it's in trouble when I see the single cross-shaped tree of the set is backed by a large screen for rear projection slides.

I really start to worry when the first slide projected on the screen is an extreme close shot of an abnormally large female breast, and a rock song by The The starts. *"Today is the day your life will surely change, today is the day when things fall into place . . ."*

The music fades out and the theatre goes dark.

When the lights come back up, Becky's sitting on the stage in a fashion-punk costume trying to take off a motorcycle boot. On the background slide the Statue of Liberty brandishes a bottle of Gallo Port instead of the torch and a cigarette is airbrushed into her mouth. Miss TV Star enters in an even more colorful costume.

The bantering of Beckett's circuitous dialogue begins:

"Nothing to be done."

"I'm beginning to come round to that opinion. All my life I've tried to put it from me, saying, Vladimir, be reasonable, you haven't yet tried everything. And I resumed the struggle. So there you are again."

"Am I?"

"I'm glad to see you back. I thought you were gone forever."

"Me too."

"Together again at last! We'll have to celebrate this. But how? Get up till I embrace you."

"Not now, not now."

"May one inquire where Her Highness spent the night."

"In a ditch."

"A ditch? Where?"

"Over there."

"And they didn't beat you."

"Beat me? Certainly they beat me."

At the right moments there's nervous laughter from the audience. Both Becky and Miss TV Star are good.

But then the slide is switched to a publicity still from a currently popular women-in-jail-taking-long-showers movie, and there's involuntary laughter from the audience. Including me.

A disaster, I think, but then Becky and Miss TV Star start getting bigger laughs off their lines.

They're playing it for every laugh they can get.

And somehow the funnier it gets the sadder it gets.

They're mocking the lines and then mocking themselves for mocking the lines.

△

During intermission I read the program. Becky, listed as Becky B. because another SAG actress uses her name, has a very simple bio: *She is an actress.* I remember how it took us a full night to write this.

I join Y.J. at the bar. He's already ordered the beers. I pay.

"What do you think so far," I ask Y.J.

"I think you should write a movie version. Don't change a word. Just set it in a high school."

"Phil Collins could do the soundtrack."

"No, Bon Jovi."

I feel the beginning of another facetious tantrum.

"Think I'll take your advice," I say, killing my beer. "And catch up on my reading in the bathroom."

The largest epithet is written in orange crayon:

EAT MY FUCK

Someone else with a black pen is a little clearer and heavier:

> "What is hell? I maintain that is
> the suffering of being unable to love."
> —Father Zossima

To which someone has added with a pencil:

> "Until I took LSD, I was incapable
> of love."
> —Cary Grant

I look back at the first scrawl, Dostoievski city, and it suddenly occurs to me the handwriting looks suspiciously like Y.J.'s.

But it couldn't be Y.J.'s because how could Cary Grant have responded. And isn't Cary dead anyway? But maybe Y.J. wrote both lines. He's ambidextrous.

No, I say to myself, paranoia is also hell, and Y.J. isn't the only person who thinks like this.

I read the dueling graffiti:

ART SAVES

A second person adds:

JESUS SAVES

A third person adds:

Because he shops at K-Mart

And a fourth sums it up with an arrow pointing to the third person's observation:

what an asshole!

And there's the honored classic:

What are you looking here for?
The joke's in your hand!

△

"I can't go on like this."
"That's what you think."
"If we parted? That might be better for us."
"We'll hang ourselves tomorrow. Unless Godot comes."
"And if he comes."
"We'll be saved."
"Well, shall we go."
"Pull on your trousers."
"What?"
"Pull on your trousers."
"You want me to pull off my trousers?"
"Pull on your trousers."
"True."
"Well, shall we go."
"Yes, let's go.
They don't move.

148

The final blackout brings a big ovation.

Y.J. and I wait awhile and then go back to what passes for dressing rooms. Miss TV Star is surrounded by hangers-on and other obsequious types who tell her how great she was.

Becky also has her share of hangers-on, but when she sees me she breaks out of the crowd and comes over smiling and reaches out for my hand. I've heard so many people telling her how good she was, all I say is hello.

There's a strange pause between us. Then she's dragged away by people complimenting her.

I sit down in a corner and for some reason start thinking about when I first met Becky and this lasts for what I think is a long time. But before I come to any big conclusions, she's standing there beside me, her hand on my shoulder.

"Let's get out of here," she says.

△

On our way out I see the guy and the girl I'd been listening to at the bar, and now they're laughing with each other. I'm glad.

Blackie is lying on the hood of the car. She gets up and barks hello when she sees us. I tell her what a great show she missed and how good Becky was and hardly wonder why I'm talking to a dog.

"It would've been particularly interesting for Blackie," Y.J. says. "She was in the original production in Paris."

"Untie her from the steering wheel," I say.

△

149

We drive into Bel-Air for a barbecue hosted by one of Miss TV Star's friends. There's valet parking. Y.J. brings Blackie as we walk through the house.

Out on the patio there are dozens of people, fewer than half of whom I saw at the play. Everyone's drinking and eating by the swimming pool as Joe Jackson screams through the huge outdoor speakers, *"The L.A. sun can turn your brains to scrambled eggs. . . ."*

But nobody's listening to Joe.

Y.J., thanks to Blackie, immediately attracts female attention. Becky and I go to the bar. She gets champagne and compliments and I get a double Scotch.

I notice two young actors holding court by a tiki torch. They're posing in the wagging tail attention of several girls, including one I recognize as a *Playboy* centerfold cum actress.

"Didn't you work with that guy?" I say.

"Once."

"Shouldn't you say hello or something?"

"Last time I said hello to him he acted like I wanted an autograph and his used shorts."

"Any luck?"

She makes a face at me. Then accepts another compliment from someone.

I spot a little guy marching through the crowd. He goes up and grabs one of the bimbos fawning over the young actors. She pulls away. The young actors both say something to their tiny rival and he suddenly swings and the actor Becky worked with takes it on the nose—his hands clap over his face and blood flows down between his fingers and into his mouth as he swears in shock.

His friend swears more loudly to attract help while maintaining a cool pose.

The little guy kicks this one in the balls, then starts swinging crazily at both the young actors' faces. Hell breaks loose as people rush over to restrain this guy who's suddenly and utterly berserk. The bimbos seem to enjoy the excitement.

A photographer is snapping away.

Y.J. comes over to Becky and me. "Lively party," he says.

"Time to make our exit," I say.

Meanwhile, Joe Jackson is still screaming through the speakers, *"Well, the Playboy centerfold leaves me cold, and that ain't 'cause I'm a fag . . . you get crazy. . . ."*

△

We come back home and eat take-in Chinese food and drink cheap sake while we watch James Stewart in *It's a Wonderful Life*.

Becky cries every time she sees this movie. I make the effort not to. I don't think Y.J. ever cries at movies.

Afterward we all go for a stroll on the boardwalk. "When things seem hopelessly confused," Y.J. is saying, "you've got to remember it just *seems* that way. Think about Blackie's situation. If I have to take her to the vet for some health problem, worms, for example, and the vet, in order to cure her, needs to keep her there overnight, well, to Blackie it just seems like senseless torture.

"I mean, she's getting needles poked into her and a gloved hand up her ass and then she's thrown in a little cage overnight. But just because it *seems* like senseless torture to her doesn't mean it *is* senseless torture. She just can't see the big picture. She may be an enlightened soul, but the fact remains she's got a dog's brain."

151

I turn to Becky. "I'm not sure," I say, "but I think he's telling us our lives are a bad trip to the vet for worms."

"Monday is coming quick," Y.J. says to himself for my benefit and his amusement.

"Look at Blackie," Becky says.

Blackie is frolicking about with a bone she's found like she's just snorted a gram of good cocaine.

"Of course," Y.J. says, "there's always the chance the animals know more than we'd ever suspect."

△

I'm lying in bed watching Becky undress in the moonlight. I'm thinking about how she looked on stage.

"You set the alarm," she asks.

"No," I say. "I'm sick."

"I know," Becky says, "but as you've said so many times—sickness is what your job is all about."

"I'm not going in tomorrow."

"Any particular reason?"

"I don't want to get up early just to get fired or quit."

"You're quitting?"

"I've been overexposed to the sickness."

She looks at me, and I can see she understands.

"I'll find another job," I say.

"I'm sure you will."

"Look at me," I say. "Wouldn't *you* hire me?"

She smiles, finishes undressing, and comes to bed and snuggles up next to me. I think about how her voice seemed different on stage. Deeper, sexier.

"God, I'm tired," she says.

152

"Go to sleep."

"I'm not *that* kind of tired."

"What kind of tired are you," I ask.

"Tired tired."

"Oh, of course."

She runs her hand down my leg. "Are *you* tired," she asks.

"Yes."

Her hand slides under the waist band of my boxers. "You don't *feel* tired."

"Well . . ."

"Where's your flask?"

"My flask?"

"Is there Scotch in it?"

"Yes—"

"Where is it?"

"It's probably in my khakis."

She gets up and checks one of my three pairs of khakis. Bingo. She comes back and kneels down next to me and takes a long swallow.

"You want any?" she asks me.

"Yes."

She smiles and starts pouring it all over herself.

"That's J&B," I say.

"It's good."

"It's expensive."

She shakes the flask empty.

"There's a bottle in my satchel," I say.

Dripping with the Scotch, she walks over to the closet and finds the pint bottle. She splashes some on herself as she comes back, then walks across the mattress and stands over me. She pours some in her mouth but lets a small stream start dribbling down her chin and down her chest and onto her stomach where the stream breaks into smaller tributaries—some of which drip off body crevices like waterfalls and others of which reach my mouth at her feet.

I lap my way upstream toward the source.

△

Afterward I find my Camels and a pack of matches. "I hope this doesn't cause an explosion," I say as I light up.

"Wouldn't be so awful," Becky says.

"*What* wouldn't be so awful?"

"To blow up right now."

Pause.

"What do you mean?" I say.

"This wouldn't be such an awful time to die."

I'm pretty sure she doesn't mean this in a literal sense.

"It would save me the trouble of finding an apartment," she adds.

I kiss her, and go to the window. She joins me.

"I wonder where the drunk with the cross is?" I say. "I kind of miss him tonight."

"It's pretty cold out there."

I notice the one-legged man and the bum sitting together on a bench. They're sharing a bottle and talking.

I explain their story, as much as I know plus my own speculation. Becky says it gives her goose bumps. I tell her she's weird.

"I love you," she says.

I never know what to say to this.

"I must have a good reason," she says. "I don't know what the fuck it *is*, but I must have one."

For the first time this week, I can't picture myself not alive.

△

Unlike Becky, I can't get to sleep.

I walk out to the kitchen naked and get a glass of water out of the tap. The Sparkletts water cooler is still empty.

The TV is on, but it's tuned to the snow between channels. I look at Y.J. and Blackie in the glow of the goonbox. They're both looking at me.

"Did you tell her," Y.J. asks.

Pause.

"I'll be back in a second," I say.

I go into the bedroom for cigarettes and my boxers. Becky, as usual, looks like an angel in her sleep. I kiss her very softly and walk out.

I sit on the futon with Y.J. and Blackie. "I'm not sure suicide is such a brilliant idea," I say, lighting a cigarette.

"Of course it's a brilliant idea," Y.J. says. "But *doing* it might not be."

"That's what I mean."

"You're bailing?"

"Not exactly."

"Then I guess I lose," Y.J. says. "How do you want to do it? Since we're doing this together, I think I should have some say. I hear you get an excellent erection from hanging—"

"—Slow down," I say.

"I don't want you to live if—"

"—Just slow fucking down."

"Okay."

Pause.

"When we were in Becky's dressing room," I say, "after the show, I was thinking—"

"I noticed."

"What?"

"You looked catatonic."

"I did?"

"You looked so fucked–up people probably thought you were an actor."

"They noticed?"

"The whole room."

"Oh."

"What were you thinking about?"

"Becky."

"Yeah?"

Pause.

"How I met her and everything. How it all started."

Y.J. nods and I start talking.

"I was alone in a screening room, watching a movie I had to write copy for. The movie, of course, was totally fucked up by Big Gun. But this one actress saved herself—Becky. I can still picture images of her from that movie. She played this small role, a debutante who somehow ended up dancing at a peep show. There was just . . . I don't know, *some*thing there.

"I got her phone number from the cast list and called her on the pretense of needing publicity information, and asked her to meet for lunch. Later she told me she was suspicious and didn't know why she ever agreed. But she did."

Y.J. is just listening.

"Anyway," I continue, "the cool sort of numbness I

usually feel in these situations wasn't there. I thought she was the most interesting, charming person I'd ever met. And couldn't figure out why. Our first night together, I remember this, she quoted something like, 'She cannot be considered as a whole. She is composed of fragments. Only passion gives her a moment of wholeness.' I said something about how I thought all actresses should have that stamped on their foreheads, and wondered to myself what the fuck I was getting into."

Y.J.'s expression is unchanged.

"You know how I've always felt about relationships, they're okay for masochists. But I started seeing Becky anyway. And it was . . . okay. We'd stay apart from each other for a night . . ." I sort of laugh. "Only because we knew it would make the next night together that much better.

"When we realized we weren't burning out on each other she moved in. Made that momentous decision while hung over on New Year's Day."

I stop like I'm finished. Y.J. still doesn't change his expression. I'm sure he knows what comes next but wants me to say it.

"Okay," I continue, "the movie finally came out and we went to see it together and I saw the big bright image of Becky B. and it seemed like someone different than the Becky sitting next to me. And the sick thing is I wanted the image."

Pause.

"Sick," I say, "huh?"

Y.J. nods.

"The Plague," I say.

"Fucked up," Y.J. says.

"That, too."

"And it's not just Becky," I say. "I do it with people in general. I'll see a girl in some kind of picturesque situation, and I'll think, 'Gee, that looks like a good commercial for Diet Pepsi.' "

"Now *that's* sick."

I nod.

"At least you're *aware* of the problem," Y.J. says.

"Wonderful," I say. "At least the guy with the big C *knows* he has it."

"Exactly."

"Excuse me," I say. "I need a drink. You want one?"

"No."

I check the cabinet. "No more Scotch," I say. "And I'm painfully sober."

"There's no way out of here," Y.J. says.

"Out of where?"

He laughs. So do I, because it's late and I know what to expect from him.

"It's ugly and getting uglier," he says. "It's cold and getting colder and there's no hope and no faith and so you have to have hope and faith or you're dead, you have to find somebody to melt with or you melt alone like the Wicked Witch in *The Wizard of Oz.*" He pauses. "Am I making myself understood?"

So much for knowing what to expect.

"We're all in the same boat," Y.J. says.

"And it's sinking."

He smiles. "You're not entitled to a movie star life."

"Of course I am."

"That's what we're told every day," he says. "We're told we're fucking *entitled.*"

"I know," I say. "I was doing some of the telling."

Y.J. nods.

"We know it's bullshit," I say.

"Do we?"

Pause.

"You have the same outs we all have," Y.J. says. "Chemical anesthesia, self-destruction, self-imposed idiocy, petty distractions, sado-masochistic relationships, and consumer hell."

"I've tried 'em all."

"Unfortunately, there aren't many other options."

"You *are* trying to talk me into it."

"I'll go with you," Y.J. says. "I always keep my word. I just want you to make a choice. Do what you think's right and ride it out."

"Now I see," I say. "You want to kill yourself but don't want to do it alone, and so you come to me thinking you can talk me into a joint venture."

"Exactly."

"I thought so."

"To even *think* of that, you have to have a twisted mind."

"Thank you."

"You're welcome."

I consider this bantering a healthy sign.

"These are strange selfish times we're living in," Y.J. says.

"True."

"You have to overcome mountains of shit."

"Large mountains," I say and flick my cigarette ashes into Y.J.'s empty wine glass.

"Don't shoot for sainthood," Y.J. says.

"Why not?"

159

"The saint is a part-time con artist. You're too concerned with details like honesty."

"Well," I say, "so much for my career aspirations."

"Forget Catholic delusions of martyrdom and just try to be a decent human being. That's hard enough these days."

"I do seem to be having some difficulties."

"I can see one possible salvation for you," Y.J. says.

"I'm not sure I want to hear this."

"It's just a possibility."

"Okay," I say. "What?"

"Beyond that door." He gestures in Becky's direction.

"Maybe?"

"Maybe."

Pause.

"Don't be an expatriate in your own life," Y.J. says.

"*What?*"

"Don't be an expatriate in your own life."

"Okay," I ask. "What does that mean?"

"Who the fuck knows?"

We both shake our heads and laugh.

"There's nothing to fear," Y.J. says, still laughing. "Except pain and misery and loss and suffering and excruciating torture on the cross of life."

"Nothing to fear."

Our laughing dies down. I put out my cigarette and light another. "Remember smoking out in the woods?" I say.

"Of course."

"And drinking that shitty wine?"

"Mogen-David 20-20."

"Mad Dog."

We cringe at the memory.

"Remember the talks we used to have," I ask.

"Do *you?*"

I nod. "And even though I go months without seeing you," I say, "I still think of you as . . . I don't know."

"Thank you."

"Your postcards never fail to amuse me."

"That's good."

"They're around here somewhere," I say. "You want to see them?"

"No."

Pause.

"I love you," Y.J. says.

Hearing that word twice in one night is a little frightening and suddenly I concentrate on my cigarette.

"Talk to her," he says.

I nod, put out the cigarette, and get up. "Good night," I say.

"Good night."

He nudges Blackie. She barks.

I walk to the bedroom door, then stop to look back.

"Possibilities," he says.

I nod and open the door.

△

She's alight in the glow of the moon, lying on her side, the white flannel sheets reaching only to the bottom of her rib cage, her breasts pointing toward the window. I watch her breathe and tell myself this image is also a person with the usual human design problems.

161

I also tell myself I shouldn't have to tell myself something so fucking obvious.

But I remember reading one of Ralph Waldo Emerson's essays about how we have to keep reminding ourselves of truths over and over and over and even if Ralph had much more grand ideas in mind it makes me feel like waking Becky and telling her everything, but she looks so good asleep I can't do it.

So I just lay myself down and hug her back.

The body is warm.

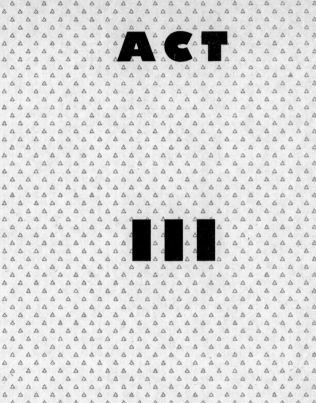

ACT III

"Wake up."

Y.J.'s shaking me, and though I can see the sunlight behind him in the window I'm sure it's not nearly time to wake up.

"Get up."

Why can't I get a decent night's sleep?

"You've gotta wake up."

"No, I'm sick."

"Come on, Blackie disappeared."

"What?"

"Blackie disappeared," he says louder. "We have to find her."

"Find her where?"

"Get dressed," Y.J. says. "We've got to find her."

"Who?"

"Blackie."

"What happened?"

"I was taking her for a walk and we got split up," he says. "I waited and called but she didn't come back."

"Maybe she got lost."

"Come on, get dressed."

I focus my eyes. Becky's still asleep. I pull on my pants.

"God this place reeks," Y.J. says. "Scotch?"

"J&B," I say. " 'It whispers.' "

"You've got a drinking problem."

"We didn't drink it."

"Then you've got some other kind of problem."

I take my pants back off.

"What are you doing?"

"I think I'd better shower."

"Okay," he says. "I'll be waiting outside."

"I'll be down in five minutes."

"Bring Becky."

"Better give me twenty minutes then."

"Hurry up."

Y.J. goes out and I kiss Becky. This doesn't magically wake her the way I'd hoped. I slap her softly and kiss her again. She flutters awake.

"Blackie's lost," I say.

"What?"

"Y.J. lost the dog," I say. "We've got to help find her."

"He lost her?"

"Yes."

"I hope she's all right."

"She's probably just playing with some of the neighborhood mutts," I say. "We'll find her."

"It smells like Scotch," Becky says.

"Sure does."

She smiles.

"Y.J.'s waiting outside," I say. "I'm taking a quick shower."

We hear Y.J.'s voice calling Blackie.

166

"I'll shower with you and save time," Becky says.

We shower together and refrain from sex—a minor miracle—and I realize this is Monday morning without the usual horror.

△

We walk the boardwalk with Y.J., calling her name.

We ask everybody, including merchants and other locals, if they've seen her. No luck. After an hour or so, we stop to think it over.

"Where would you go if you were a dog," Becky asks.

"She likes playgrounds," Y.J. says.

"There's a playground off Lincoln Boulevard," I say.

△

A group of young kids, black and white, are playing two-on-two basketball while their girls hang out and watch, but no dogs. I start to drive away.

"Hold on," Y.J. says. "Let me ask these kids." He jumps out of the convertible and jogs over there.

Becky and I stay in the car.

"You ever play any sports," I ask her.

"*Sports?*"

"Like girls' basketball or anything?"

Becky just looks at me funny.

"That's a normal question," I say, "isn't it?"

"Girls played a *different* kind of sport where I grew up," she says and smiles.

"Boys."

Becky nods.

"I never really played any sports," I say. "Not any

team sports. Skiing and tennis were fine, but I could never seem to get along in the others."

"I can think of one team sport you excel at."

Before I can comment, a Fine Young Cannibals cover of the Elvis classic "Suspicious Minds" comes on the radio and Becky turns it up and sings along, *"We're caught in a trap. . . ."*

Watching Y.J. talk to the kids on the basketball court, I have a strong yearning for the purity of a twenty-foot jumper. I want the life of a Magic Johnson or a Larry Bird. I want to play in a game with clear rules and a scoreboard and male bonding in the showers and a girlfriend with rubbing alcohol at home.

I wonder if after having a forty-point game Larry Bird loses sleep pondering the suffering and sadness and madness and terrifying confusion of human existence? I doubt it.

I imagine the rush of a game-winning three-point swish. Fuck cocaine.

Alas, I'm afraid love is probably the closest a sedentary chain-smoking, substance-abusing, sport-drinker like myself can come to purity or perfection.

I'm thinking about the connection between championship rings and marriage rings and rings around the collar when Y.J. returns to the car.

"One of them *thinks* he might've seen her around here earlier," Y.J. says.

"What now?" I say.

"We keep looking."

I realize that someday I'll have to wrestle with this three-ring concept. But not today.

△

We're driving around when Y.J. spots some dogs on a side street. "Turn left!" he shouts. I turn before I realize we're going into an area generally avoided by sane or unarmed citizens.

Halfway down the block there are six or seven young Mexican men in suspiciously similar outfits sitting on an old car on a dead lawn. There are a couple canines hanging out with them.

I can either throw it in reverse, thereby looking suspicious as well as ridiculous, or I can drive on and hope our ignorant arrogance will save us from attack. I choose the latter course and pray they won't mistake us for that loathsome media myth, the fucking yuppies.

"Slow down," Y.J. says.

"What," I say and keep driving, feigning deafness or idiocy.

"Here!" Y.J. shouts. *"Stop!"*

Now I'm sure the whole neighborhood's listening and looking, so I give up and stop.

"Hey," Y.J. says to the gang, "any of you guys seen a white dog that looks like a coyote running around here?"

I look over. Nobody seems to be going for their guns. They look at each other and shake their heads negatively.

"No, man," one says, "but the dog catcher's been hanging around here the last couple days."

"Check with the pound," says another.

"They nab free dogs, man."

"Thanks," Y.J. says.

I start driving away.

"Fellow dog lovers," Y.J. says.

△

The howling and barking and whining is disturbing Becky, so I'm glad when Y.J. comes out of the animal shelter and gets back in the car.

"The trucks are checking back in about an hour," he says. "Let's go see if she's returned to your building."

"I guess we just hope they caught her," Becky says.

"No," Y.J. says, "we hope they *didn't.* They might not let her go."

"Of course they'll let her go," I say as we drive away from the animal noises. "You'll just have to pay a small fine. *I'll* have to pay a small fine."

"Blackie has a record," Y.J. says.

"What?"

"A criminal record. They were going to put her to sleep."

"For *what?*" Becky says.

"When I first got here, I took her out by the ocean, and we were walking by this beach club and Blackie smelled a barbecue from about two hundred yards away and, well, I guess she was hungry so she ran over and snagged a steak. And," he says, "the weird thing is she's a vegetarian."

Becky and I look at each other.

"They're not going to gas a dog for grabbing a steak," I say.

"The guy doing the barbecuing had a conniption fit and attacked her with this hot poker he was using on the coals. She defended herself, naturally, and bit him. Then all these men in La Coste shirts got into it."

"They ganged up on that sweet animal?" Becky says, and I try to figure out when she became so fond of the beast.

"Blackie nipped a few more, I guess," Y.J. says.

"By the time I got there the beach Animal Control people had a rope around Blackie's neck. The beach clubbers wanted her to be declared a public menace."

"A public *menace?*"

"Something like that. Anyway, I had to beg and con the Animal Control people to give her up. I made all sorts of impossible promises—like I would keep her on a leash."

"Do you even *have* a leash?" I ask.

"No," Y.J. says. "But I talked it over with Blackie, and she said she'd rather take her chances."

"Of course."

"So you think if they catch her, they'll really put her to sleep," Becky asks.

"They might try. If it's the same outfit."

We search the streets all the way back to our apartment building, where we stand outside and wait while Y.J. calls for her. There's neither hide nor hair.

After an hour or so, Y.J. starts to lose his voice and so we drive back to the animal shelter.

"I'm sure they'll release her," Becky says. "We'll just talk them into it."

"We're semirespectable people," I say. "They might listen to us."

We arrive and Becky and I want to go in with Y.J., but he insists on going alone. Becky urges him to let her help. I tell Becky Y.J. knows what he's doing.

So she and I sit in the car and wait for him while the dogs howl.

"What am I going to do?" I say. "For a job?"

"You'll think of something."

"Like what?"

"You tell me."

"I don't know."

"It's going to be okay," she says. "Now relax, it's your first day of unemployment. Enjoy it."

I turn on the radio and try to enjoy. KROQ is playing the Bangles' "Manic Monday" as they seem to do every Monday lately. But this is the first time I've heard it with dogs howling in the background. From now on the song probably won't sound right *without* the dogs.

Y.J. returns to the car with a big smile. "They have her," he says, his voice thoroughly raspy.

"Yeah?" I say.

"She's on death row."

"Death row."

Y.J. nods, still smiling.

"Why are you smiling?"

"I know what to do about it."

"What?"

"I cased the place," Y.J. says. "We bust her out tonight."

"You're suggesting that we break into an animal shelter."

"Yes."

"I see."

"You don't have to help," Y.J. adds.

"We'd love to help," Becky says.

I look at her and she smiles. I shrug in return.

"Good," Y.J. says. "I'll stay here and case this place a little further. You might as well go to Big Gun and clear your life out of there."

"Now?" I say.

"Now is as good a time as any."

"Now may be a good time for *some* things, like getting drunk, having sex, and so on, but—"

"—I'll see you back at the apartment in a couple hours," Y.J. says and walks away.

I turn to Becky. "You really want to do this?"

"We *have* to."

"Y.J. could manage by himself," I point out. "He's highly capable."

Becky just stares at me, not amused.

"Okay," I say.

Pause.

"Guess I'm going to Big Gun now," I say.

"Want me to come with you?"

△

We ride up the elevator.

"This is really interesting," Becky says.

"Not really," I say.

"It *is*," she says. "You had this whole life here I didn't really know much about."

"I wouldn't call it a whole life."

"Five mornings a week."

"More like three and a half, on average."

We get out of the elevator and I lead her down the hall toward my office. The hall seems strangely deserted, but absentee rates at Big Gun are generally very high on Mondays. Wendy and Susie and most of the art department are probably still sleeping off the weekend.

"Incredibly ugly carpet," Becky notes.

We come to Angie, the receptionist. "Hi, honey," she says. "Wild weekend?"

"Yes," I say. "Angie, this is Becky."

"Hi," Angie says nicely.

"Hello," Becky says.

"Should I tell Peg you're here," Angie asks.

"No," I say. "I'll be gone again in a couple minutes."

Angie laughs.

I lead Becky on into my office and close and lock the door behind us.

"This is really interesting," Becky says.

She's looking around. There's not much to see. No photos, nothing on the walls, just my desk, my type-writer, and my telephone, and the sticky yellow notes stuck up everywhere.

"Doesn't look like anyone really works here," she says.

"No one really does."

Becky goes to the window and admires the view of the smog.

I rummage through my desk drawers. Broken pencils, liquid paper, 8x10 glossies, notes, articles I've clipped, rotting granola bars, aspirin, Tylenol, Nuprin, Valium, Juicy Fruit gum, promotional buttons for movies, files of my worst work, phone numbers written next to names I don't recognize. I take Y.J.'s "intricate rituals" postcard and decide to leave everything else.

I walk over and stand with Becky. "When I first got this office," I tell her. "I felt very adult."

She laughs.

"Really," I say, "I thought coming to an office like this made you an adult."

"You didn't realize it could just as easily make you a sleaze bucket?"

"Ward Cleaver was no sleaze bucket."

"*Who?*"

"Ward Cleaver. The Beav's father."

Becky nods. "What are you going to do with yourself?" she says.

174

There's a knock on the door. My first thought is to run for cover, but obviously there isn't any.

Becky looks at me.

"Yes?" I call out.

"Zeke?" It's Peg.

"Maybe," I answer.

Becky looks at me, apparently amazed I said *maybe*. I gather my wits and unlock and open the door.

Peg steps in. "Are you okay?" Peg says, then notices Becky.

"Peg," I say, "this is Becky."

They say hello to each other.

"Peg's in charge of advertising and marketing here," I tell Becky.

"Oh," Becky says.

Peg looks like she needs a lithium really badly.

"Could I see you in my office?" Peg says to me. "I'd like to discuss your *T Team* copy."

"No."

"Pardon?"

"No," I repeat, "I'm leaving now."

"You just got here."

"I just came back to pick up my stuff," I say. "But there's nothing here I want."

Pause.

"I'm quitting," I say because she looks confused.

"What?" Peg says. She isn't sure whether I'm joking.

Becky and I walk out, leaving Peg standing there looking out toward the smog and probably still wondering if I'm joking.

△

When we step out of the elevator into the parking

175

garage, Wendy and Susie are stumbling off of Susie's scooter. They're either still drunk or wickedly hungover. They don't see us, and I lead Becky off in the opposite direction. We circle around to my Rambler, which is conveniently parked in a spot reserved for Big Gun's owners.

As I start my car a red Mercedes sedan pulls up alongside. It's the fattest of the three owners. And sitting with him is a movie star.

The star broke into the business by writing and starring in a small movie that was said to have heart and soul. It did. And it still made millions. Now the star's making more millions by writing, directing, and starring in big-budget exploitation flicks about the joys of burning and murdering your fellow man. An *auteur*. Big Gun, who claim they can't afford to pay their employees union wages, have just signed a six-million-dollar deal with the star.

"Bela Lugosi's dead!" I yell as I back my car out.

They look at me strangely.

Becky and I laugh.

△

We're driving down Pacific Avenue in Venice.

"I'm hungry," Becky says. "Let's have lunch."

"We're almost home."

"I hear there's a tremendous new little Mexican place in the marina," Becky suggests.

"Who's going to pay for it?" I ask.

"Visa?"

I shake my head.

"Am Ex?"

I shake my head. "We've got to stop spending money we don't have."

"Why?" Becky says. "It's so much *fun*."

Pause.

"Okay," she says. "Let's go to a grocery store."

△

In the check-out line I pick up *Time* magazine. "I'm fascinated by *Time*," I say.

Becky smiles and picks up *People*.

I skim an essay about the fifteen-year Me Decade finally ending. The essayist believes America is poised for a new beginning. Sounds good, but you wouldn't know it from reading the *Time*-owned *People* that Becky is leafing through and laughing at.

△

We pick up Y.J. and go to the ocean and drink wine out of paper cups. I don't know if it's the paper cups or what, but the cheap wine tastes excellent.

The afternoon wind picks up and it feels good.

We sit in the sand on the edge of the tideline and plot the mission of Blackie's liberation until the sun sets.

△

Back in the apartment, Y.J. takes the phone into the bedroom while Becky and I watch *Bonnie and Clyde* on the VCR as a kind of a joke to prepare for tonight's breakout.

Y.J. joins us just as Warren Beatty shoots the man with glasses in the eye and we decide to send out for pizza.

I'm into both the pizza and the movie when there's

177

a loud obnoxious knocking on the door. I hit the VCR pause button and go over to open the door.

It's Wendy and Susie. "We're early," Wendy says. "Aren't we?"

I don't know what Wendy's talking about.

"We *wanted* to be early," Susie says, "to make up for missing your last party."

I don't know what Susie's talking about either.

"Hi girls," Y.J. says.

Wendy and Susie come in and Susie hands me a six-pack of Trident Subs. Minus the two she and Wendy have in their hands.

I look at Becky so she'll realize I don't know what the fuck is going on here, but she looks like she *does*.

"We didn't know how to dress for a nuclear Armageddon party," Susie says.

"So we dressed like always," Wendy says.

"We're *always* dressed for Armageddon," Susie says.

They are indeed dressed as usual, Wendy in all black and Susie with her icons, but I still haven't any idea what they're talking about.

"I wanted it to be a surprise," Y.J. says.

"Good work," I say.

"It seemed like a good idea," Becky says. "Since you weren't feeling so well for your birthday party. Think of this as a second-chance birthday party."

Y.J. and Becky smile at each other.

"What do you think of the theme," Y.J. asks me.

"Touching."

"I think it's real ballsy you quit," Wendy says.

"I wish I could," Susie says.

"Don't worry," Wendy says to Susie, "you'll probably get fired eventually."

"Yeah," Susie says. "Now that Zeke's gone, it's really going to suck." She turns to Becky. "We just *love* Zeke."

Pause.

"Wendy, Susie," I say, "I don't think you've ever met Becky."

They all shake hands.

"We've heard you're wonderful," Wendy says.

"I've heard some interesting things about you, too," Becky says with a smile.

"They're all true," Susie says.

Much to my amazement and relief there are no cat hisses. Becky shows no malice, and Wendy and Susie show no shame.

"You're watching *Bonnie and Clyde*," Susie says, staring at the video, which is still on pause.

"Yes."

"Way cool," she says, "let's watch the ending. I *love* the ending."

"Okay."

Just as I start the tape there's another knock on the door, so I put the tape back on pause and go to answer it.

It's Bob Cutler. "Hi, big guy," he says.

"Come on in,' I say.

"This is how I'd dress for nuclear Armageddon," Bob says, dressed in his normal business suit.

Bob's eyes bulge when he sees Wendy and Susie. Introductions are made and we sit down to watch the orgasmic blood bath of Warren Beatty and Faye Dunaway.

△

By midnight a couple dozen people are babbling and drinking to beat the band and Prince is playing *"We're going to party like it's 1999 . . ."*

179

A few wear costumes, a tin-foil suit being the most notable, but most people are dressed in their usual clothes with the simple excuse that this is how they expect to be dressed when the big moment comes.

I'm standing alone with a Scotch thinking about how nobody here except Y.J. knows about the strange see-saw trip I've been on the last few days and that, I think, is the way it's supposed to be.

I wonder now if maybe I blew it.

But what can friends do when you announce you're in a spiritual crisis and feel intensely suicidal? Besides act facetious and laugh because nobody's supposed to give a fuck anymore. And I want to shout Fuck you.

And instead I laugh and hope it helps.

"What's so funny?" Susie says.

She and Wendy have sidled up next to me and both are staring at me.

I shrug and smile.

"Come on," Wendy says.

Wendy and Susie each take an arm.

"Come on where?" I ask.

They take me toward the bathroom and though I neither need nor want drugs, I come along peacefully.

"She's *beautiful*," Susie says after closing the bathroom door. "And not beautiful like an actress, but like a human."

"We like her anyway," Wendy adds.

"She seems like a, I don't know, *nice* person," Susie says.

Wendy pulls out her little packet of coke.

"Don't you feel sort of silly running into the bathroom like this?" I ask.

"Yes," Susie giggles.

"No," Wendy says and starts unfolding the paper.

"Are we still going to be acting like this ten years from now," I ask. "Can you picture us doing this in our *thirties?*"

"How depressing," Susie says.

"Sneaking into bathrooms and coming out numb," I say. "Coughing up phlegm balls."

"The phlegm balls are the *worst,*" Susie says.

Wendy opens up the paper and smiles fondly at the coke. "You can always wash out the phlegm balls with Scotch," she says and dips her black-painted fingernail into the white powder and then up at my nose.

"You know," I say. "I really don't want any."

"No?"

"No thanks."

"Really?"

"Really."

"Come *on,* Zeke," Susie says.

"You *know* you want it," Wendy says as she teasingly wiggles the loaded fingernail in front of my nose.

"No," I say. "I just came in here to . . ." I don't know why I came in here.

"To snort this coke," Susie says. "To kill the pain."

"To kill the pain?" I say and laugh.

"She's right," Wendy says, still taunting me with her offering. "The painkiller's on its way."

"Take it," Susie says.

"Uh-oh," I say. "Peer pressure."

Susie laughs. Wendy keeps waving the fingernail.

"This is going to sound like kind of a wild idea," I say, "but do you suppose there's some other way to kill the pain? Other than making ourselves temporarily dumb and numb."

181

Pause.

"No," Wendy says.

"No," Susie says.

"You're probably right."

"I guess there's sex," Susie suggests.

"Besides sex," I say.

Wendy puts the fingernail to her own nose and whiffs. This makes her smile. She reloads her fingernail.

"What keeps you from committing suicide?" I suddenly ask.

"Now that's a *weird* question," Wendy says.

"Not *that* weird," Susie says.

"Well, okay," Wendy agrees.

Pause.

"What keeps me from committing suicide?" Wendy repeats.

"Yeah, and you too, Susie."

Wendy and Susie look at each other and laugh. *"We* don't fucking know," Wendy says.

"I know," Susie says, raising her hand.

"Yes?"

Susie suddenly looks sad. "Oh," she says, "I don't know."

"What were you going to say?" I ask.

"It'll sound stupid," she says. "I don't know what it *is,* but I'm sure that if I did it it would sound stupid." She giggles. "Maybe I'll write a poem about it."

Wendy offers her a fingernail full of cocaine. Susie doesn't seem to notice.

"Maybe I could get a job as a teacher," Susie says.

"What?" Wendy and I say at once.

"I could get out of the biz," Susie says. "And start teaching kids about art or something."

"That's a frightening thought," I say, picturing her *T Team* poster and other such masterpieces.

Susie grins.

"Here," Wendy says, shoving her fingernail up toward Susie's nose, "you need this."

Susie stares at the coke and shakes her head.

"What are you shaking your head for?" Wendy says.

"I think Zeke just spoiled it for me," Susie says.

Wendy looks like she's about to go into severe shock. "What's *wrong* with you two?" she finally says and starts to pull her fingernail away.

But Susie grabs Wendy's hand and puts her nose to the fingernail and sucks it all in with one mighty snort. "Sorry, Zeke," she says, wiping her nose, "but I've been looking forward to this all night."

Someone knocks on the door.

"Occupied," Wendy calls, then loads her fingernail and pushes it toward me. "Last chance."

I have many happy associations with little mounds like this one. Many ugly associations also.

"Well," I say, "maybe for nostalgia's sake." I start to lean down—

"No," Susie screams mock melodramatically, "don't do it!" Susie grabs me, and Wendy pulls back the fingernail and spills the contents all over her leather pants.

"Shit," says Wendy.

Susie and I are laughing and touching. I'm sort of glad she grabbed me.

There's more knocking on the door.

"Occupied," Wendy shouts, wiping the coke off her pants and licking her fingers.

"I should get back out there," I say.

Wendy puts the packet back into her purse and we open the bathroom door and there's Bob, smiling to let us know he knows. We smile back.

As Bob steps into the bathroom Wendy says, "Oh, I forgot something," and steps in with him and the door closes.

Susie and I look at each other and shrug.

"You weren't serious about that, were you?" I say. "About becoming a teacher."

"I don't know," Susie says. "Ask me next week."

Now that I've quit Big Gun I feel like I'm going to have two good friends in Wendy and Susie. It's a good feeling. A week ago this thought would've scared me shitless.

"I think I better drink something to kick back that coke," Susie says.

We look at each other and laugh, then Susie wanders off to the kitchen and I join Becky and her agent, Tina.

"I'm starting to seriously question what I'm doing," Tina is saying as she sips her white wine and smokes her Virginia Slims. "I'm working way too hard for such a fucking trivial game."

Becky sips on her own wine.

"But don't worry," Tina says, "you won't need to start looking for a new agent. Every once in a while I think I'm accomplishing something." She smiles. "And I like the perks."

I walk away to the kitchen to get myself a drink. Bob and Wendy come up as I'm pouring myself a Scotch. They both smile at me like co-conspirators. Bob starts mixing a couple G&T's.

"It's really weird," Wendy says loudly and rapidly

to Bob. "I've always had this vague feeling I've been *cheated* out of something, you know, something I'd been promised."

I remember telling Wendy this exact thing last week. But she sounds serious.

Bob nods and concentrates on the gin-to-tonic ratio.

I decide to wander around the party and eavesdrop aimlessly, and eventually find myself next to Susie, who's talking to a guy Y.J. and I went to school with.

"You remind me of the father on the 'Brady Bunch,' " Susie says. "That's the kind of life I've always wanted."

The poor guy thinks she's kidding.

Over by a window, Y.J. is chatting up Mary Stuart, Scott, and Noni, people from Becky's acting class. Whatever it is he's saying, they look hooked.

I wonder what Y.J. is going to do with his life. For the first time it occurs to me that maybe he's already doing it.

Some drunk guy I don't know comes up to me and says, "Swingin' party," and I wonder if he's making a reference to The Replacements' song.

The festive rites of futility continue, and I'm both observer and participant in sundry conversations about all the ailments of the age.

Fear of commitment and fear of not making a commitment and fear of sex diseases and fear of bizarre death and fear of fear and fear of confusion and confusion of fear and confusion and fear of all the favorite fears and confusions.

It's a good party.

△

Y.J. and Becky and I slip out unnoticed. As we walk down the hall I can hear R.E.M. on the stereo. *"We have hope despite the times . . ."* and I wonder if my neighbors like the music.

I really should find out who they are.

△

As soon as we pull into the parking lot, a couple of the dogs start howling and barking.

"They're going to go nuts once we get in there," I say.

"Let's go," Y.J. says.

He gets his tools out of the trunk, wire cutters and a crow bar, and the three of us run over to a six-foot wire mesh fence topped with barbed wire. Y.J. starts snipping a hole in the fence, and I whistle a few bars from the theme song for "It Takes a Thief." Then we climb through the hole into the courtyard outside the main kennel.

The cages are designed so half the cage is inside the building and the other half extends outside. By now all the dogs in the outside section are barking and howling at us and one of the dogs is Blackie. She's jumping around her cage in ecstasy, as if she knows perfectly well what's happening. Y.J. says hi, and jogs around to the shelter entrance and starts jimmying the door with the crow bar.

Becky and I throw biscuits to shut up the beasts. Our plan works amazingly well.

"Ohhhhh," Becky says, "look at this sweet animal."

Becky is feeding extra biscuits to a small dirty blonde puppy who looks part Golden Retriever.

"How do you like prison?" Becky says.

The dog whimpers in response. Becky melts. She looks at me and I know what she's thinking.

186

"No," I say.

Becky's pout mirrors the puppy's.

We hear Y.J. open the main door, and we run around to follow him inside. He quickly sets to work on Blackie's cell door.

Becky and I survey the inmates. Some are full-grown mutts and others are puppies that will grow up to be mutts. They're all looking at us with a mix of wonder and hope. Some slumbering atavistic instinct comes alive inside me and I suddenly want to set them all free.

But the rational self says, no, they've nowhere to run. They'll just starve or be smooshed by speeding cars.

Becky gets on her knees and starts baby-talking to the dirty blonde puppy. "Were you a naughty boy?" she says.

The puppy is wagging his tail no.

Y.J. snaps open Blackie's cage door and in a shot she's out jumping and slobbering all over him in thanks.

"Let's go," Y.J. says.

He and I look at Becky, who is still kneeling on the floor. "Don't you have any family or friends to bail you out," she asks the puppy.

The puppy whimpers no.

Y.J. goes over and reads the data sheet on the cage. "They picked him up more than a week ago," he says. "If he isn't claimed in a couple more days, he's dead meat. Either that or fodder for animal experiments."

Becky looks up at me.

"Do we *really* want a puppy?" I ask.

Becky's eyes say yes.

"Free the furball," I say to Y.J.

△

187

We return to the party with Blackie and the puppy. The animals immediately hog everybody's attention and revel in it like drunk debutantes.

Somebody tries to get the puppy stoned by blowing smoke in his face, and I step in to play good father and suggest he's a little young to be debauched.

When I think the pup's partied enough for one night, Becky and I take him for a walk with Y.J. and Blackie.

Blackie runs into the water, up to her knees. The pup tries to follow, but clumsily retreats every time a new wave comes in and wets his paws.

Standing with Becky and Y.J., at the edge of the ocean in the moonlight, seeing my friends in the light of my window and watching the animals frolic in this enormous sandbox, I feel like running around and jumping up and down.

I don't, of course.

But feeling like I *could* is enough.

△

On the way back in, we stop to get our mail. There's just one letter. It's from my life insurance company.

"I wonder what they want?" Becky says.

"I asked them to send me some forms," I say.

"For what?"

Y.J. starts whistling.

"Nothing important," I say. "I'll show you later."

As we come down the hall I can hear music pouring from our apartment. Someone nostalgic for the seventies has put on one of my old Elton John albums. *"Goodbye yellow brick road . . ."*

We enter the din.

"You're just in time for *Beer Hunter!*" Susie shouts.

Becky goes into the bedroom to prepare a bed for the puppy. Susie makes Y.J. and me stay.

Wendy and Susie are organizing a game of Beer Hunter with the brave souls still partying. The first-round players are Wendy and Bob Cutler. As in the Russian Roulette scene in the movie *The Deer Hunter,* the two players sit across from each other Indian-style complete with bandannas. Between them are placed six Trident Sub beers. One of the tall boys is thoroughly shaken up and mixed back in with the others. This is the loaded can.

Bob goes first and points a beer at his head.

The crowd quiets.

Bob pops the top and a little beer drips out. He swings the can to his mouth and guzzles it and the circled crowd cheers.

Wendy then places a beer to her head. She pops the top with the same effect. She drinks it down much slower than Bob, but gets a fond round of applause anyway.

Bob picks up a third can and aims. He starts laughing and pops the top—it explodes—he's soaked. The first casualty. The crowd laughs and Bob drunkenly laughs harder.

Bob goes into the bathroom, followed closely by Wendy.

Susie takes over and decides Y.J. and I are next. Becky comes back from the bedroom just as I'm sitting down across from Y.J., who picks up the first can. He points it at his head and closes his eyes and pops the top. Nothing. He guzzles it and the crowd cheers dutifully.

I pick up a can and glance at Becky. She rolls her eyes.

I pop the top. Nada. I hand the beer to Y.J. and *he* guzzles. The crowd loves this improvisation.

Y.J. does it again. Again nothing. He hands me the beer and I guzzle it.

I go through the motions with a fresh can. Still no action. I hand it to Y.J. and he polishes it off.

The cheers quiet quickly. Only two cans remain. Y.J. smiles. The crowd starts a soft chant, "Beer Hunter, Beer Hunter . . ."

Y.J. picks up the can and points it at his temple.

The crowd quiets.

Again nothing happens when the top is popped. I take his can and slowly drink it down.

The chant starts to build, "Beer Hunter, *Beer Hunter, BEER HUNTER* . . ."

I stand up and toss Y.J.'s empty across the room— *swish* into the sink.

And then I bow out.

The beer-thirsty crowd responds to my resignation with mocking moans until Y.J. snags the loaded can and starts spraying everyone. "You want beer!?" he shouts, "*I'll* give you beer!"

Insanity rules as people arm themselves with beer cans and return fire.

And Elton John is singing, *"I've seen that movie, too . . ."*

△

By two A.M. the partyers are mercifully gone. The mess remains. Becky and I and Y.J. and Blackie sit on the futon and watch a tape of an old "Twilight Zone."

Richard Basehart and Elizabeth Montgomery play two astronauts from separate unnamed countries stranded

on a strange new planet because everybody on the unnamed planet they come from is either dead or mutated
from nuclear war. They don't get along at first, Montgomery beans Basehart on the head with a rock, but eventually
they work it out. Richard Basehart's character is named
Adam. Elizabeth Montgomery's character is named Eve.
The two decide to call the strange new planet they're
stranded on Earth.

Afterward we make the usual complaints to each
other about how superficial the new "Twilight Zone" and
"Amazing Stories" are and turn on the stereo.

△

My favorite old Bowie tune is playing. *"Though
nothing, nothing will keep us together, we can beat them, forever
and ever, we can be heroes, just for one day. . . ."* and my arm is
around Becky and I feel okay and I'm thinking I should
outgrow this song and wondering if I ever will.

"Fidelis ad urnam," Y.J. says.

I nod.

"Remember what that means?" Y.J. asks me.

"No."

Y.J. smiles and winks and I know he'll be gone in
the morning.

He can go fuck with someone else's life.

△

It's after three A.M. and the full moon is beaming
right into our bedroom. Becky and I are standing at the
window looking out. We can hear the waves coming in.

She's holding the life insurance papers I showed
her when I confessed.

"You wouldn't have really done it," she says.

191

"I don't know."

"How?"

"I was seriously considering drowning, but—"

"How could you not talk to me about this!?"

Pause.

"What was going on in your head, Zeke?"

I keep gazing out the window. "I'm not sure I can say."

"What were you thinking?"

"I guess it was more just the way I was feeling."

I can feel her eyes on me.

I start talking, "The night of my birthday party . . ." I tell her the story. What I see and what I feel and the things and the Plague and so on. I try to tell the truth. I also try to summarize, knowing she's bright and can fill in the blanks, but it's getting light out by the time it's all been said.

She hasn't spoken a word.

And now she's staring at me like I'm insane.

"I was sort of numb," I say. "It didn't seem like that big a deal."

"Killing yourself? That didn't seem like a big deal?"

"We're all headed there anyway," I say, "I was just thinking about taking a head start."

"For chrissakes, Zeke." She shakes her head. "What did you think would happen when you died?"

"I don't know," I say. "I think that was part of the appeal."

Pause.

"And you thought I'd say, 'Too bad about Zeke killing himself, but at least he left me *money*.' "

"Not exactly," I say, "but I thought you could use it. The money."

"That's sick."

"Yes."

"And what about the guilt," she says. "What about the *guilt?*"

"I was going to leave a note absolving you."

Becky looks incredulous. "What the fuck kind of note could have absolved me," she asks. "You think you're *that* good a writer?" Pause. "So what were you going to write in this note."

"I don't know," I say. "I didn't get quite that far."

"Where do you *get* these ideas?"

"I don't know."

Pause.

"But it got us here," I say.

"Where? Where are we now? I've got an unemployed suicidal boyfriend."

I laugh, but Becky doesn't.

"You wouldn't really have done it, Zeke?" Her voice has changed a bit.

"I didn't really *want* to," I say. "I was looking for a reason *not* to."

"And?"

"And what?"

"You didn't say if you found one."

"Yes."

"What?"

"What?"

"What is it? What's your reason not to?"

"I told you."

"When?"

"I told you the whole story. Everything. Well, everything except what I didn't tell you, but that would just be more of what I did tell you."

Pause.

"And hey," I say, "the search goes on."

Becky frowns. "You mean you can't think of a reason not to . . ."

"I mean I feel like I'm beating it now," I say. "I feel like I have some faith in something."

"What?"

"What do I have faith in?"

"Yes, *what?*"

"Well," I say, "you and me, you know, whatever's between us."

She sighs and bites her big lower lip.

I toss my cigarette out the window and watch it twirl through the dark and when it lands on the boardwalk the glowing ember explodes into a spray of sparks that fade.

"You ought to put my name down here as the beneficiary," she says, gesturing to the insurance papers. "Just in case."

She almost smiles and I laugh.

"You were very good tonight," I say.

She looks at me.

"You raided that animal shelter like a real warrior. And you handled Wendy and Susie quite well."

She just looks at me.

"I don't tell you much," I say. "About the way I feel. But I do admire you, you know."

"I don't want you to admire me," she says. "I just want you to understand."

Not knowing what to say, I say, "I'm sorry."

She doesn't say anything.

"Want to kill me," I ask.

"No."

"Mace me?"

"No."

"Maim me?"

"No."

"Want me to tie you up?"

She smiles, and I feel a whole lot better.

But I suddenly go from feeling better to much, much worse—almost nauseous. "God, I'm sorry," I say.

"I know."

And suddenly we're holding onto each other and I'm crying and feeling a little silly about it and it occurs to me I haven't cried for years, which just makes me gush some more and we're kissing as we cry and, realizing this, we start laughing.

"There's a dog trying to climb my leg," I say. "He better not take a leak."

"*Look* at him," Becky says. The puppy's wagging for attention.

"When I was about six my mother gave me a puppy," I say. "I was too young and irresponsible to feed it, so my mother did all that. Naturally this made it like my mother was better than me. So I took it down to the basement and put it in the dryer—one of those big dryers with windows. I watched the puppy go round and round until I got bored and went to my room."

Becky is horrified. "Did it die," she asks.

Pause.

"Of course it died," she says. "Why are you telling me this?"

"So you won't send me out to do laundry with the puppy."

Becky looks up and shakes her head. But then she laughs. "I love you," she says.

"I know."

She rolls her eyes.

"I love you," I say.

"I know."

"You're not going to leave."

Becky shakes her head and we look at each other and then we both look out the window at the smog-blue light of the coming sunrise. I reach over and hold her hand. The puppy jumps up on her leg.

"Let's take the pup for a drive," she says.

"Now?"

"Why not?"

"Okay."

We both get down on our knees to play with him.

"It's a strange, sick world," I tell him. "Just don't chase any cars."

The animal seems to understand.

Mark Lindquist lives in Venice, California. This is his first novel.